Where Have All the Tigers Gone?

Where Have All the Tigers Gone?

LYNN HALL

CHARLES SCRIBNER'S SONS / NEW YORK

This novel is a work of fiction. Names, characters, places, and incidents are either the product of the author's imagination or are used fictitiously. Any resemblance to actual persons living or dead, events, or locales is entirely coincidental.

Charles Scribner's Sons Books for Young Readers
Macmillan Publishing Company, 866 Third Avenue, New York, NY 10022
Collier Macmillan Canada, Inc.

Printed in the United States of America
First Edition   10 9 8 7 6 5 4 3 2 1

Library of Congress Cataloging-in-Publication Data
Hall, Lynn.
Where have all the tigers gone?/Lynn Hall. — 1st ed.   p.   cm.
Summary: En route to a high school reunion, a fifty-year-old woman, now a successful novelist, reminisces about the personalities and relationships in her class and about her own feeling during her school days of never fitting in.
[1. Self-perception—Fiction.   2. High schools—Fiction.
3. Schools—Fiction.   4. Friendship—Fiction.]   I. Title.
PZ7.H1458Wf   1989   [Fic]—dc19   88-28835   CIP   AC
ISBN 0-684-19003-6

Where Have All the Tigers Gone?

I went out after supper to drape myself over the corral fence and enjoy the twilight with Pauncho. In the morning there would be time enough only for chores before I left to drive down the mountains into my past.

My life had distilled myriad acquaintances into a handful of close and treasured friends, human and otherwise. Pauncho was the most daily of my friends—he and Theo, who would be taking care of him in my absence. And George, of course, my dog. Beyond these three, there were two or three writer friends with whom I exchanged letters and books, a couple of women friends here in Pine, and that was it.

To people out in the real world, with circles of friends from school or work or clubs, my life probably seemed sparse and lonely. It was not. It fit me.

I turned and leaned my shoulder blades against the

corral's top rail, arms outstretched along its splintery length. Pauncho's rubbery lips brushed my arm, played at my shirt collar. His teeth snatched at my hair. I whammed him in the chest with a backward karate chop and he jumped away from me.

As always, when I was about to leave home for a business trip or a speaking tour, my love for this little valley intensified to the point of pain. I'd heard it said that people never cry from joy, not really. They weep not for the good they have now but for the lack of it that they formerly suffered. A woman, hearing "I love you" from the man of her choice, grows teary-eyed because of all the I-love-yous she longed for in the past and didn't get. I ache with the love of my home, my life here, out of fear of losing it, out of remembered need for it when I didn't have it.

The valley was tiny, a high, shallow depression in the upper slopes of the Sierra Ancha mountains, sixty miles north and east of Phoenix. The soil was Arizona-red, but at this elevation it grew pine forests and lush grass, not the sage and cactus of the lower valleys. Days were dry-hot, but the night air was fragrant and cool, even now in August.

My house stood before me and to the left, a rambling log thing centered around a huge rock fireplace. It had been a one-room cabin when I bought the place eighteen years before. I'd built the two new wings myself, with help from Theo and Ginny and a how-to book. It was my home, deeply and purely. I intended to live out my life in it, die in it, and have it burned down after me so I could take its ashes to heaven when I went.

Sighing with contentment at what I had and a soft sadness at leaving it even for a few days, I ducked through the corral rails and wrapped an arm around Pauncho's chest for a mutual lean-in. It was the way we hugged.

He was a short, stocky dun gelding, cream colored with brown stockings, mane and tail, and brown stripes over his withers and down his spine. I'd bought him as a green-broke three-year-old the year I'd come here. His name was Pancho then. The paunch came with middle age. Paunches—his and mine. He was twenty this year, I was fifty: both a little thick through the midsection, neither ready to slow down.

As I stood leaning against my horse, wondering if there would be time to get the saddle out and grab a quick ride before dark, I felt his head jerk up. I turned and followed his gaze to a bulky shape trudging up the road. Theo. Hers was the only other house in our tiny valley; the road led in from Highway 87, past her little blue cottage, and dead-ended in a red dust turnaround in front of my house. We had worn a permanent path through the grasses and wildflowers, a straight shot from my door to hers. Hers and Ginny's, until two years ago. Now just hers.

I left Pauncho with a slap on the brisket and went to meet her. Theo. Dear friend. The words were hardly adequate.

She was older than I by ten years, a tall, thickly built woman who seemed to be growing shorter and broader every day since we buried Ginny. Her hair was a wild mop of iron gray, sometimes lassoed into a ponytail, sometimes uncontrolled around her shoulders. She wore slacks always; on top, tentlike garments in Indian patterns and colors; on her feet, Hopi moccasins. In her mouth, always, were the small dark cigarillos. They weren't really cigarettes, she used to say rather foolishly, so she wasn't really smoking.

George appeared from somewhere and gallumphed to meet her. He was a Bernese mountain dog, a black bear of a creature with tan and white markings on face and feet. My Christmas present from Theo and Ginny, six years ago.

We met on the footpath with a tangle of golden August weeds catching at our shoes. Our greeting hug was wordless, automatic, but mutually nourishing all the same. She bent to rumple George's ears, then we walked on toward my house, arms around each other, moving in unison, liking the warmth of a friendly body in uncomplicated closeness.

"You're still going," she said darkly.

"Of course."

We mounted the porch steps and went inside. The sun was down now and the air suddenly too chilly for comfortable porch sitting. We went into the lighted kitchen, just off the main room, and Theo settled on a stool to watch me start coffee. I'd lit the fireplace just before I went outdoors; its mesquite-fragrant warmth was close to us, beyond the counter that divided kitchen from main room.

My house was unashamedly corny-western. Longhorn antlers hung over the doorway, woven Indian totem mats on the walls, Hopi kachina dolls on shelves in the

4

corner. Indian rugs covered the plank floors, their earth colors echoed in the blankets that covered sofa and chairs. My dishes were heavy pottery.

For a kid from the suburban Midwest, I'd evolved a long way into the fantasy life I'd chosen for myself.

Beyond the main room, to the far side of the fireplace, was the bedroom wing built by me and friends. It was rough hewn and low beamed like the rest of the house, and it held my work area as well as my solitary sleeping place.

There, on plank work tables, were the computer and the stacks of reference books and completed manuscripts and jacket sketches and editorial correspondence that supported my life here. On a shelf over the work space stood a long row of my books, each one a three-month chunk of my life. *Badlands War*, by J. J. Herne, *Rimrock Raiders*, *Death in Sagebrush Canyon*. And farther down the shelf, *Love's Flaming Fury*, by Jessica Heather, who was also J. J. Herne, who was also Jo Herne: me. A plain old fifty-year-old gal from Des Moines, Iowa, living out a happy pretend life in western shoot-'em-ups. I threw in an occasional romance if I needed extra money for repairs around the place, but the westerns were my love.

I poured the coffee, ripped open a bag of nacho Tostitos, and the moveable feast shifted to softer perches in the living room. My coffee table was a huge log split lengthwise and laid on legs of smaller wood chunks. Corny, sure. I loved it.

Theo sank deep into the sofa, feet on the log table, one arm around George, who had climbed up beside her to watch each Tostito from bag to mouth. I settled in my saggy ranch-oak easy chair, put my feet beside hers, and took a pull of coffee.

"You're really going," Theo said again, this time with glum acceptance.

"Look," I argued patiently, "it's a direct flight, Phoenix to Des Moines. No crowded airports. I don't have to go through Chicago or St. Louis or Denver this time. Just a simple hop, here to there."

"Pilot-error crashes happen in small airports, too," she said, blowing cigarillo smoke away from me. The draft from the fireplace blew it back.

"Flying is still safer than driving," I reminded her. "You're getting to be a regular death's-head about this flying stuff, Theo. I wish you'd knock it off. I have to travel in my work, I always have, always will. So lighten up."

"Yes, but this isn't work," she said heavily. "This trip you don't have to take, you know. What's a high school class reunion anyway? I never went to any of mine and it never hurt me."

I swallowed an impatient retort. Since Ginny's death, Theo had grown increasingly dependent on me. She and Ginny had loved each other truly and deeply for more than twenty years. The worst of the mourning was past now for Theo, but much of her strength and optimism were buried with Ginny, and now her biggest fear was of losing me, too, and having no one.

She had never flown and distrusted planes and pilots, so every trip I announced upset her. Now I drove to writers' conferences and speaking engagements when I could; but this trip was fifteen hundred miles to Des Moines, Iowa, for two days of high school reunion. Driving would have taken a full week of time I needed to finish the revisions on *Riders at Dawn*.

"Class reunions are stupid, anyway," Theo muttered.

"Well, maybe. Still, I want to go this time. I missed the last one, and this was such a weird class that they may never have another reunion. They had one at twenty-three years and now this one at thirty-two. Don't ask me why. Normal classes have them every five or ten years. Not us." I chuckled a little and went on.

"Actually I didn't *miss* the first one, I just didn't bother to go. I never liked school. I had less school spirit than anyone in that place. Oh, I got good grades, it wasn't that. But I was, I don't know, just out of it. I hated the way I looked; I had crushes on just about every boy in class, and none of them could see me for dirt. I didn't even have a date for my own senior prom. Isn't that pathetic?"

Theo barked her deep laugh. "Neither did I. Neither did lots of perfectly good people, if the truth were known."

"Isn't it interesting how people turn out?" I said idly. "I mean, the ones who seem so enviable in high school might screw up their lives with bad marriages, drugs, whatever, while some of the ones nobody ever noticed in school go on to become . . ."

"Famous authors."

"Right. Rich and famous authors of deathless prose living in regal splendor in mountaintop mansions."

We grinned at each other.

7

"So, that's why I want to go to this reunion. So I can gloat and show off."

"And to see how everybody else turned out," Theo said.

"Right. And to hope all the women are wrinklier and saggier than I am, and all the guys who wouldn't ask me out are now fat, bald jerks."

I took from the table the high school yearbook I'd been leafing through that morning and shifted over to the sofa, beside Theo and George.

"Let's see what you looked like," Theo grunted.

The yearbook was black leatherette with white lettering. *Tiger Tales.* White line drawings of the school building and a prowling tiger filled the cover. *Valley High School. West Des Moines, Iowa. Class of '55.* Such a nice round number. I'd always liked that number. It was the year of my release from that building, that constricted part of my life.

Yet here I was, actually looking forward to going back, to seeing all those people again. But of course I was going back as a success. Quiet, out-of-it, clumsy Jo Herne had become this successful, happy, confident woman, and I wanted to show her off.

"That was me," I said, pointing to a picture of a lantern-jawed, dark-haired girl wearing a short-sleeved, pale sweater and single-strand pearl choker. Her eyes were focused at the designated spot over the photographer's left shoulder, her arms arranged in fictitious langour over the back of a chair. Her hair was short, combed straight down from a side part, curled up tightly around the bottom and across the forehead. It was the

8

worst possible style for my long, rawboned face; it was the same style two-thirds of the girls' pictures showed— except that on mine there were uncontrolled wisps of hair showing along the neckline.

Theo stared at the picture for a long time and browsed on. "That one looks jolly," she said, pointing.

"Roberto Rodriguez. The class clown. He was one of the dumb kids, but he was nice. Jolly."

The face above Theo's broken fingernail was a circle full of circles: double chins, round eyes almost hidden by grin-lifted cheeks, a spill of curly, black hair above the low forehead.

"You had Mexicans in your little Iowa suburb back in the fifties?" Theo asked, mildly surprised.

"A few families. I think they'd come up to work on the railroads early in the century and stayed on. West Des Moines started out as a railroad town called Valley Junction, before Des Moines became the state capital and grew out around it and turned it into a suburb. When we lived there it was just a nice small town, with open fields between it and the big city of Des Moines. Now it's an elite suburb with a classy antique shopping mall called Valley Junction. Full circle.

"There were a few Mexican families, a few black families. They had their own little neighborhoods, kind of hung out together, you know, but I was never aware of any problems. I remember how surprised and upset I was when I got older and found out about prejudice. To me, those kids had been just another clique that I didn't belong to.

"You remember how it was in school. There were all

those layers! There were the top layer, the ones who were class presidents and glory athletes and committee chairmen. And then there was the next level down, the ones who hung out with the top-level kids and actually did most of the work on the committees and were going steady by tenth grade and never had to worry about anything. And then there were all the other subgroups. The one I was in—oh, maybe six or seven of us—was the girls who got reasonably good grades but never had dates. And there were the genuinely pathetic ones, the fat ones, and her"—I pointed to another picture— "Hazel Stott, the class dog. And there were the Mexican kids and the black kids. We all had our own . . . level. I wonder if we chose them for ourselves or if they somehow got assigned to us. I can't remember now.

"This one was my best friend," I said, pointing again. "Charlotte Yoder. Strange person. We didn't have a thing in common."

"Did you keep up with her after graduation?" Theo asked, digging into her moccasin to scratch at her instep.

"Nah. Well, yes, for a while. I took off right after I got out of school. Went to Denver and lived with my older sister for a while. Her husband was stationed there in the air force. I told you all about that chapter in my life. Charlotte stayed in Des Moines, got a job, got married, had kids. It was what she always wanted. I've often wondered how it actually turned out for her. We wrote letters for a while, then just Christmas cards. Not even that, for a long time. I wonder what she's like now."

"What was she like then?" Theo asked. One of her most endearing qualities was her unfailing interest in me and my life.

I chuckled. "She was a blob. A blah blob. No personality, no opinions. I was the chief, she was the Indian. I've often wondered what kind of wife she made. She'd never argue with anyone. I'd think she'd be boring as hell to live with, but there are probably some men who would think that was great. No power struggle."

"That one looks like she's got a bad smell up her nose," Theo said with a snort. The picture was of an elegant face, smooth, blond hair in a shoulder-length bob. Haughty eyes, no smile.

"Patricia Winston. I hated her," I cackled. "I really want to see how she turned out."

"And hope for the worst," Theo nodded.

"You betcha."

/ • /

By eight the next morning I was wheeling the Blazer around the curves of narrow Highway 87, descending by loops from stark brown slabs of mountains into boulder-strewn foothills, then across high flatlands patrolled by twenty-foot-tall cacti.

Usually this drive excited me. Even after all my years in Arizona, I still fantasized Roy Rogers and Gene Autry galloping in hot pursuit of the bad guys, with Trigger sliding down canyon walls and kicking up dust billows in his wake. I'd spent the best parts of my childhood with an ear to the radio, listening to west-

11

ern adventures and drawing horse pictures on pads of typing paper.

But today I barely noticed the movie-set scenery around me. Almost automatically I drove down and down, to the edge of the city and around it to the airport. I sat bemused in the waiting area and boarded my plane with barely a glance at the other passengers.

I settled into my seat, arranged my too-long legs, and buckled myself in. Leaning back, I closed my eyes and saw, more clearly than I had for decades, those faces in the *Tiger Tales* yearbook.

Patricia, whom I envied blackly with no clear understanding of why she was superior to me and why her life was charmed.

Hazel Stott on the opposite end of the spectrum, for whom I was grateful, ashamed of feeling that way, but grateful for someone to whom I was clearly superior.

Bruce, the childlike face on the third page whom I hadn't pointed out to Theo; Bruce, who should logically have been my first love.

Laughing Roberto, who gave dumb answers in class to make us laugh.

And Charlotte. My best friend.

My eyes stayed closed through the flight attendant's explanation of flotation safety devices, through the roar and liftoff, and opened only long enough to accept a small plastic glass of diet Coke from the beverage cart when it came.

Charlotte Yoder. Best friend. What an empty travesty of friendship that had been, compared with the depth and strength of friendships I'd known since then. Charlotte and I had never connected at all. Why were we coupled in best-friend status all those years?

How on earth had we begun?

=/ 2 /=

I was nine the summer we moved to West Des Moines. We had been living in a small town up north, near the Iowa-Minnesota border, where Daddy had been second man in a two-man city water department. Life had been comfortable and familiar for me there. I had my established slot in the social structure at school, and I knew where all the horses lived, around the edge of town.

The move to a city suburb scared me. The fact that adults kept assuring me I'd soon make new friends alerted me to dangers I hadn't considered before. Friendships had never been one of my worries; friends were there from early on, like neighbors and family. Now suddenly parents and aunts and teachers were patting me on the shoulder and telling me how easily I'd make new friends in West Des Moines. If they were that concerned about it, I reasoned, then it must be a hard, scarey thing to make friends in a new school.

I didn't want to leave Kendallville, but Daddy had a chance to be the top man in the water department in West Des Moines, and that was supposed to give us a better life, so we moved.

Our new house was bigger than the old one in Kendallville, and it was nicer. Even I could see that. It sat on a corner just one block away from Main Street, where Daddy's office was located. The house was tall, steep looking, with white shingles and blue shutters, no porches to speak of but with a collar of shaped bushes around its foundation. The huge garage had once been a barn for carriage horses; that fact alone endeared the place to me.

The other winning feature was the number of bedrooms; there was one for me and one for my older sister, Jeanette, even one for three-year-old Judy. For the first time in my life I had space of my own and a door to shut out intruders. With that, I figured I could live happily in this new town, friends or no friends.

I was "shooting" farm animals in my room on a rainy afternoon a week or so after the move. The original plan for the afternoon was to continue my systematic exploration of the streets of West Des Moines. I'd gone out several times, walking a different way each time, trying to find the edges of the town and, I hoped, a pasture with a horse in it. So far all I'd found were more blocks of streets.

But rainy days were good, too, if you had your own

room. That afternoon I was simultaneously enjoying three of my best things. One was a small suitcaselike record player that played one 78-rpm record at a time. I owned two single records, a Gene Autry and a Sons of the Pioneers, and a three-record album of Gilbert and Sullivan operettas given to me by an uncle who understood me better than anyone else.

The second prized possession was an old mattress from a youth bed. I don't know what happened to the bed or how I came to inherit the mattress, but it lived under my bed and was dragged out for use as a luxurious floor mat. I spent much of my time standing on my head on the mattress, feet braced lightly against the wall. I didn't take seriously Mom's warning that my brains would all run out my nose. I liked looking at things upside down, and I liked the challenge of balancing on the teetery surface of the mattress. I also liked the security of knowing I'd land in comfort if my balance failed.

That afternoon I lay belly down on the mattress, listening to Gene Autry sing. I was in fact a keen-eyed sheriff lying high on a rocky bluff and drawing a bead on the procession of cattle rustlers riding into the canyon below.

The rustled cattle were the six model-farm-set cardboard cows propped up on flimsy bases. The farm set was my third best thing. The red barn fascinated me with its horse stalls and hay wisps and harness drawn onto the cardboard walls. I loved setting up its fences and arranging the animals, even though I was probably too old for such a toy.

My trusty six-shooter was a rubber band looped under my curled little finger, stretched around behind my thumb, and hooked over the tip of my pointing finger. Take aim at the black Angus bull, release little finger, *powee,* one dead bad guy.

I set up the row of targets again and got comfortable on the mattress, behind the outcrop of mountain boulders, always wary of the death-warning buzz of rattlers in the sagebrush. Just as one was about to strike, my stallion, Fury, had killed it for me, chopping it into a gory mess in the dust with his iron-shod hooves.

I was singing along with Gene when the bedroom door opened. I turned to see Mom standing there, with a strange girl behind her.

"I found you a new friend," she said brightly. "I was just over at Schultz's and I saw somebody who looked like she'd be about your age, so I invited her home to meet you."

I cringed inside. My mother was dragging people home from the neighborhood grocery store and forcing them to be friends with me. The humiliation was overwhelming. This girl half-hiding behind Mom didn't want to be here any more than I wanted her to, and besides that, she was going to tell everybody in the new school that I couldn't get friends on my own. I had to have Mommy snatch them for me off the streets and out of the alleys.

Mom maneuvered the girl through the doorway and left us to each other, saying, "Her name is Charlotte, she lives just over on Seventh Street, and she's going to be in fifth grade with you when school starts."

17

I crawled over to the record player and lifted the needle off of Gene. Then I stood, needing to meet this new person on her level. My first reaction was, she's no threat, although I didn't analyze the notion of threats in newly met friends.

She was shorter than I, rather round of face and limbs, with mid-brown hair rain-plastered to her skull and hanging in thin, wet worms around her neck. Heavy glasses rode too far down on her nose. She wore saggy shorts of a faded cotton print and a blouse with puffy short sleeves and untucked tails. She stood on the sides of her feet, rocking from one to the other. In her arms was a small brown bag from Schultz's Grocery, with a loaf of bread leaning out at the top.

"Hi," I said. I couldn't think of anything else.

"Hi." Her voice was soft and high, babyish.

It occurred to me that she was scared of me. That was a new experience. I'd often tried to scare my baby sister into doing what I wanted, but she had a direct line to Mom, the ultimate protector. Here was a whole new person standing there sizing me up while I sized her up, and somehow managing to send me signals that strengthened me, that granted me power over her.

She smiled a wet-lipped little smile and her eyes shifted away from mine.

"Put your bag down," I said, and she put it down.

I did a quick collapse into an Indian-style cross-legged sit on the mattress and after a hesitation she sat, too, more awkwardly.

"Did my mother really get you out of the grocery

store and drag you home, like you were a cabbage or something?"

I didn't mean that she was like a cabbage. It was just that the humor of the situation had broken through my initial embarrassment, and I needed a giggle.

Charlotte turned bright red. Like a tomato. She said with just a trace of a lisp, "Your mom just asked me what grade was I in and did I live around here, and I told her; and she said you just moved to town and didn't know anybody, and would I come over and play with you. So I came over, but I can't stay. My mom sent me for bread and hamburger, and I've got to get home with it."

Because I couldn't think of anything polite to say and didn't want to tell her I was happier playing by myself, I showed her my stuff. Sixteen model horses ranging from bronze-cast western horses with key-chain reins to cheap black plastic trotters with hollow undersides; rows of my own drawings of horses, done in colored pencil and carefully taped to the closet door because tape was forbidden on wallpaper. My cowboy boots with the glow-in-the-dark Tom Mix spurs that cost fifty cents and five Wheaties box tops.

She said, "You must like horses."

Mentally I raised my eyebrows at her intelligence and said politely, "Sure. Don't you?"

She shook her head and sent water drops sailing through the air. "I never thought about it."

"Then I don't suppose you know of any horses that live around here, close enough to walk to."

She looked at me with a glimmer of superiority and said, "Don't you have a bike?"

"No. Not yet. But I'm going to get one," I invented quickly. Her glimmer died and I felt a drop of meanness in my soul.

Then I felt irritation at her for being so feeble that she made me treat her that way. Some friend, Mom. Go back to the store and see if you can find me a riper one.

Oh well, I thought as I walked Charlotte politely down to the back door, when school starts I'll find a good friend. If I decide I need one.

/ • /

The elementary school was three blocks from my house, one block west to Seventh, where Charlotte lived, then two blocks north. It was a forbidding building, gray concrete with curved corners and glass-brick windows on either side of the main door. Inside were shiny brown tile floors in the halls and green walls. The rooms were all around the outer edges of the building, with a gym in the center.

I'd been there a week before with Mom, when she signed me up as a new kid. The principal, Mr. Lane, had talked to me for several minutes, not about school stuff but about my interests: horses, cowboys, and horses. He was a slim, tidy man who moved like a dancer, and he'd poked at my sense of humor until I'd laughed with him.

Still, on this first day of school, I approached the building feeling very much like a convicted horsethief going to jail. I walked with Charlotte, who was not at all afraid. Of course she wouldn't be. She was going back to something familiar. I wouldn't have been afraid if I'd been going back to my old school; reluctant to give up my freedom, but not afraid.

Fear was too strong a word, really. There was an underlying dread of being stared at as the new kid, and there was the uneasiness of not knowing the building. Beyond that was just the September ache of confinement away from the outdoors that was my natural habitat. When I'd started first grade I'd been afraid of being unable to learn along with everyone else. The mystery of reading had loomed over me, a puzzle too big for my small brain. But the code had been broken, letter by letter, and I'd found to my surprise that I was one of the smart kids.

Now the work I'd be doing in fifth grade didn't intimidate me; but the other kids did. I'd have to find my level among thirty strangers.

During the past two weeks, since Mom had picked Charlotte out of the fresh produce for me, I'd spent most of my afternoons with her. I'd rather have played alone or read. I'd found the town library three blocks from home and was absorbed in a wealth of horse books that I hadn't read before.

But Mom stood behind me gently wringing her hands over my solitude and saying, "Go outside and play with your new friend. Don't be a hermit."

The trouble was, Charlotte and I couldn't find much common ground. Her disinterest in horses was evident and she didn't seem to have any special loves of her

21

own. She took accordion lessons, a point of superiority over me, but she never played unless she had to, and I never listened unless I had to.

Her house was smaller and poorer than mine and held two noisy younger brothers. I didn't like it there. There always seemed to be a faint odor of unchanged diapers in the air, and the clutter and noise depressed me.

Sometimes we borrowed or stole her brother Joe's bike and pedaled side by side through the quiet, shady streets of West Des Moines, enjoying the speed of our wheels and imagining that people who saw us were envious of our soaring freedom. We went to the town park or to Charlotte's grandmother's house or to the edges of town looking for horses. And so the days passed, and a friendship of sorts began.

By that first morning of school, Charlotte had claimed me for her best friend. I could see no other girl in her life that I might be displacing, and I realized that she must have been without a sidekick before I moved to the neighborhood. Sensing that her need to be paired with someone was greater than my wish not to be paired with her, I walked willingly enough into our new classroom in the role of Charlotte Yoder's best friend.

The teacher was my least favorite kind, a heavy older lady with hairs growing out of chin moles and a glaring lack of humor. She would teach us our fifth-grade stuff and make us behave, I sensed, but she would give us nothing important of herself.

We were allowed to choose our own seats that morning, to be sorted later, with the nearsighted and the troublemakers in the front. I grabbed a window seat near the back, and Charlotte followed me. Inside the desk were my books for the year, last year's abuse mended and erased. The desk top was scratched and inked with initials and symbols of individuality. I began immediately planning where my JH with a horse head around it would go.

I spent a great deal of time that first morning studying the faces of the other twenty-nine. We were an even thirty, five rows across, six seats deep. I was far enough back to see most of them without moving my head very far.

I was startled at first to see four brown faces and three black ones. In Kendallville the differences among the pupils had been only hair color and sunburn. Now, for the first time, I could see real live black people up close. I was fascinated. There were two girls and a boy, and they seemed exotic to me, aloof and superior. They looked at me with disinterest, from behind curtains in their eyes, and I knew instinctively that I was of no use to them.

The Mexican kids were different. They seemed to radiate self-confidence and a kind of merriment that was strange and attractive to me. At least, two of them did. A chubby, curly-haired boy in the row next to mine and a very pretty girl beyond him seemed to be sending out twinkle-shoots from their eyes. The other two Mexican boys were in the far corner and I couldn't see them as well. For the two within my range I felt a warm kind of curiosity. I sensed that they would talk to me, play with me at school, although they wouldn't let me further than that into their lives.

Among the other faces in the room were a few interesting ones, a few that might become best-friend material. I skimmed past the boys. They were a breed almost as separate as the black kids. I sorted the girls and eliminated several. The fat ones, the messy-poor, were filed in my mind on a level lower than mine. Two or three were filed higher. One was a blond girl with classically even features and a withdrawn, almost bored expression. Patricia, her name was. There were two darker-haired but equally pretty girls, obviously Patricia's friends, and I lumped the three of them together on the highest shelf in my mental filing system. They were beyond me, above and beyond.

One face caught my attention and held it. It was an odd face. The phrase "homely as a mud fence" came to mind. She was a little childlike girl, with dull, dark hair that frizzed out from her face, and skin the color of oatmeal. Her teeth were splayed outward slightly, separated in the middle by a space almost big enough for another tooth. Her eyes were small dark beads, close together, and her eyebrows were a stern dark line straight across her face, fading slightly over her nose. I felt sorry for her, but I knew she would not be my best friend.

My friend would come from somewhere in the middle range of girls. She'd be bright but not show-offy, and she'd love horses and reading, and she wouldn't be hanging around all the time when I didn't want to be hung around.

I made these assessments during the morning while Mrs. Gray gave us lengthy and pointless descriptions of the textbooks in our desks and told us what we'd be learning during the year. Shut up and get on with it, I thought more than once during her monologue.

Late in the morning Mr. Lane came into our room, bouncing on his tiptoes as he walked. "Sorry to interrupt," he said to Mrs. Gray, "but I have a welcome gift for our new girl."

Moving swiftly, he picked up a stick of chalk and began drawing on the far end of the blackboard. I knew right away what it was. Horse ears, the line of the head, eyes and nostrils not quite where they should be, swirls of mane and curves of prancing legs. Under the horse he wrote, "This is Joanne's horse. Do not erase."

My grin was partly embarrassment at being singled out for attention, but mostly delight. What an incredibly kind man, for a principal. What a perfect gift. He made me feel special in the good way.

A note came across from the chubby Mexican boy next to me. I unfolded it in my lap and read, "I like your horse. Roberto."

I slipped the note into my arithmetic book as a little spot of tangible warmth, and I sent a grin over to Roberto. He made a face and rolled his eyes, and somehow made me feel that he understood my new-kid strangeness and was telling me he was on my side.

I relaxed a little, then, and set my mind to the task of paying attention to Mrs. Gray's drone.

/ • /

As the school year progressed the friend groups within our class began to jell. There were five of us in my group: Charlotte and I, Carolyn, Diane, and Shirley. We all lived within a five-block radius and we all fell roughly in the mid-range among the girls in 5-B. There were two other fifth-grade classes, A and C; but we weren't in daily contact with them as we were with our own class, and they remained strangers unless the lines were crossed by cousins or next-door neighbors.

Carolyn was the leader, a tall, strong-voiced girl who always knew how the Saturday afternoon should be spent. She had straight, brown hair chopped off at ear length, and eyes that met mine with a direct, almost challenging stare. She made me think of a warrior in search of a foe.

Shirley was the silly one who said dumb things, possibly on purpose because she felt that was her role. She wore her yellow hair in sausage ringlets like Shirley Temple and told us Shirley Temple was her cousin. No one believed her. She lied effortlessly and often.

Diane was thickly built and colorless, both physically and mentally. She was the only child of older parents who ruled her every move. She was quiet, passive, willing to do whatever Carolyn wanted. When I began to be absorbed by the group, Diane made it very plain to me that she and Carolyn were best friends. She sat or stood close to Carolyn and stared distrustfully at me until it became clear that I respected her possession of Carolyn.

Shirley and Charlotte seemed sometimes to pair off,

26

but Charlotte preferred me, attached herself to me whenever she could, for no reason that I could understand. I wasn't especially nice to her, and Shirley was.

Charlotte leaned on me. I hated it but didn't know what to do about it. During most of the time we spent together, I would have preferred to be in my room reading or off around town, exploring alone. None of these girls sparked that special interest in my mind. They were okay, they were probably the group I belonged in, but they were . . . ordinary. I found in none of them an imagination that worked the way mine did.

Carolyn came closest, and in fact I liked her best of the four, but she seemed content with Diane as a best friend and had no need of me. Carolyn was obsessed with sports. She had her own basketball hoop on her garage and when she wasn't directing us in boring ball games she was drawing chalk lines on the cement and seeing who could jump farthest. It was always Carolyn.

My birthday, in October, yielded the much-needed bike. I'd been allowed to pick it out at the hardware store, tell the store man which one I liked best, then pretend to be surprised when I got it. I picked it because it was so different in color, a pale blue trimmed with cream stripes. All the other bikes in the store rack were hard, dark blues and reds. Mine was different, and I loved it for its individuality all the years I rode it.

With the bike for my friend I began slipping away from the other girls when Mom thought I was with them, being properly sociable. I explored farther into the countryside and discovered horses to visit.

About three miles north of town there was a

paintless, weedy riding stable that I discovered on one of my explorations. I bent every effort toward making friends with the man who ran the place, so that I could trade a Saturday morning's labor, cleaning stalls, for an hour's ride on a rental-ruined horse or pony. Then winter closed in and Saturdays became bedroom days again.

Television was spreading slowly through middle-income families, but it wasn't in ours yet. I didn't miss it. I had my radio, a brown plastic box that brought me wonderful Saturday morning programs: Roy Rogers and Tom Mix and Gene Autry, the Cisco Kid and Pancho. "Ho, Cisco!" "Ho, Pancho!" Laughter and galloping hooves fading into imagined distances. I lay on my shoulders on the floor mattress, legs and body up the wall, arms flung outward, mind absorbed with the radio stories.

Something very much like romantic urges were beginning to stir in me. The idea of a boyfriend grew gradually, from ridiculous to faintly desirable. Of course, he wouldn't be like anybody at school. He would live a tough outdoor life on horseback, with a yellow scarf at his neck and a real leather vest. Or he would wear soft green-plaid flannel shirts and ride through a forest, loving me deeply and automatically.

We celebrated Valentine's Day in 5-B, in the accepted way: Everyone gave everyone a valentine. But there were gradations. There were the stock cheap ones that came in big books, like coloring books, and were cut out and assembled and given to people who didn't

28

mean anything to you. There was a bigger one for Mrs. Gray, with "teacher" somewhere in the message.

Then there were the more personal ones made in art class for people who were special and needed the distinction of a better card. I gave much thought to that category. Charlotte would have to have a personal one, I knew. By this time she had claimed me publicly as her best friend and there was no way out of giving her a special card. But I balked at the idea. She wasn't special, not to me, not in any way at all. I hadn't kicked free from her yet only because no one better had come along and it was too much bother.

There were people in the class to whom I wanted to give special cards, with whom I wanted to make contact. Foremost was Roberto, who continued to fascinate me. He got grades that were among the worst in the class, but I sensed that there was a good brain in there, behind the sparkling eyes and chubby cheeks. More than once I'd felt that he knew the right answer when Mrs. Gray called on him, but that he'd given a wrong, silly answer to make us laugh. I didn't understand why he was that way, but I liked him—flat-out, plain old liked him.

I wanted to give him a handmade card, but I didn't. There was that invisible space between the Mexican kids and me, and I didn't know if it could be stepped over. I felt I'd be an intruder if I tried.

Mary, the Mexican girl, was another I wanted to honor with a special card, and it would have been slightly more acceptable in her case, since she was at least a girl, like myself. She was a clown along with Roberto, but a bright one who seemed to be fully accepted by everyone in the room. She led committees and gave funny speeches and simply . . . bounced. But I shied away from her because she was too special. Her self-confidence swamped mine. I felt that she would receive overtures of friendship from me cheerfully, as she would from anyone. But we could never be close friends. That was understood by both of us, and not mourned.

I was tempted to give a special card to Hazel, the homely-as-a-mud-fence girl, but I was shy of her. She was quiet to the point of invisibility, and I was afraid of approaching her. She seemed hard-shelled and self-reliant behind her poor face. And to have Hazel for a friend would be a violation of the strata that existed in that room. I would be jumping boundaries as clearly as if I'd approached Roberto or one of the black girls.

So Hazel and Mary and Roberto got silly safe valentines cut out of the book.

I ventured one stroke of boldness that day, a handmade valentine to Bruce Whiteside, who had moved to town during the winter and relieved me of the label of newest kid. Bruce was very small and childlike, with a narrow-jawed face and shy, deerlike eyes. He dressed more neatly than any other boy in the class, and he was quietly, timidly bright.

Bruce was nothing like my imagined boyfriends in leather vests and plaid flannel shirts, but he was superior in 5-B, and I felt an affinity with him although we seldom spoke to each other.

Via the white-covered cardboard box on Mrs. Gray's desk I sent Bruce a handmade valentine that said, "Welcome to the newest boy from the newest girl. Joanne Herne." It was hardly a passionate love note, but he blushed as though it had been. Although he didn't look over at me when he read it, his ears burned red most of the afternoon.

I followed him out of the room at the end of the day and saw him drop all of his valentines, including mine, into the waste can in the hallway near the main door.

I felt thrown away myself.

/ 3 /

There was a period, during the summer before seventh grade, when Shirley made a serious attempt to take Charlotte away from me. She told Charlotte lies about me, made up insulting things I was supposed to have said about Charlotte. I hadn't said them, but oddly enough they were things I'd thought. I was smarter than Charlotte; I didn't like her hanging on me all the time—that sort of thing. Shirley may have been more astute than any of us realized.

But the tactics failed. Charlotte confronted me, I told her the truth, and together we turned against Shirley. "Liar, liar, pants on fire," we yelled at her, and she faded out of our group.

I was a little surprised at myself for defending my property with such feeling. I still didn't actually like Charlotte, but I wasn't going to stand still for having her taken away from me. More and more, as we grew up, the girls of our class drew into pairs. Even the undesirable had best friends, but not Hazel Stott. We did things in twos or fours or sixes, and I coasted along with the others, unwilling to make the emotional effort of being a loner, unable to find a mate who suited me better, and yet essentially separated from the need for pairing as I saw it in Charlotte, in Diane, and even in Carolyn.

On an early morning that August, I pedaled past Charlotte's house on my way to the riding stable. It was going to be a hundred-degree day, and my plan was to get the three-mile bike ride out of the way before midmorning, stay in the cool of the stable as long as I could, then take it easy on the ride home. I hoped to go alone, because the stable was my place, not Charlotte's nor the others', but she was waiting for me as I coasted past her house, and fell in beside me.

Although she had no interest in horses, Charlotte seemed to enjoy tagging along with me to the stable. Boys were sometimes there on the long summer afternoons, and she flirted with them in a breathless, tense way.

As we coasted, sweating, into the stable yard, I could tell that Bill wasn't there. His battered, green stock truck was missing. Bill Whitaker was fat and bald and loud, and he was my friend. He was semiretired from a used-car business and ran the stable as a money-losing hobby. The property had been sold to a housing developer who would tear down the stable that winter and bulldoze the riding rings.

The stable already sagged, as if it didn't mind going to its death. It housed eight or ten common-looking horses, two or three ponies, and a tackroom full of battered western saddles. The horse population constantly shifted as Bill bought and sold, so I had learned not to attach myself by the heart to any of them.

Charlotte and I parked our bikes under a shade tree and went into the cool dimness of the barn. A strange man sitting on a straw bale looked up at us. He was small, elderly, unshaven, with a ring of grease around the band of his western hat. And he was smoking.

"You're not supposed to smoke in the barn," I told him. "It's against the rules."

He looked me up and down, and instinctively I drew back closer to Charlotte. "Who do you think you are?" he asked. "You want to rent a horse, or you want to tell me my business?"

I looked at him silently. "Where's Bill?"

"Gone down to Missouri to a horse sale. I'm in charge, if you want something." His hard little eyes glittered at me.

Charlotte whispered, "Let's go."

I could sense her uneasiness without turning to look at her. But I had pumped and pedaled three miles for my horseback ride, and I wasn't backing down now.

"I work here," I told the man. "Bill always lets me ride for an hour if I clean stalls for two hours first. And I get to brush any of the horses I want to, except the stallion."

He looked me up and down again as though measuring my muscles, but this time a small grin pulled his lips

34

to one side. "Honey, if you want to shovel horse manure all morning, that's fine by me. I'll just watch. Don't get to see too many pretty girls around here. I always like to watch a pretty girl, especially in shorts."

I carried jeans and western boots in my bike basket, for the horseback riding, but wore T-shirts and old shorts for the hot bike ride and stable work. Now, with the man's eyes on me, I wished for the jeans.

"Let's go home," Charlotte said more urgently. The man's eyes were on her, too, and the smile still creased his stubbled cheeks.

"I want to ride," I insisted under my breath.

She stayed as close to me as possible while I pitched rank straw from one stall after another and replaced it with clean bedding. Twice I almost impaled her on the tines of the pitchfork as I swung my load onto the waiting wheelbarrow.

When the phone rang and called the man away momentarily, she said, "Jo, let's get out of here. I don't like this guy. He's creepy, the way he looks at us."

"He's harmless," I said. I really wanted that ride, and I'd earned half of it already. "And besides, there are two of us. Two against one. He couldn't hurt us. And he wouldn't, anyway. Bill wouldn't hire anybody to run the stable that wasn't okay."

"Don't go off riding and leave me here alone with him, will you?"

I paused in my pitching and looked at her. She was genuinely afraid. Now that her body had started rearranging baby fat into breasts and hips, Charlotte's natural modesty was becoming almost hysterically defensive.

I was no longer allowed into the bathroom with her, and when we spent the night together she undressed in hiding. My own feelings on the subject were much more casual, but even I felt the prickling of distaste on my skin when the old man looked at me.

Still, today was my only chance this week to ride, and I thought of the woods trail with longing. I'd just begun to be genuinely good at sitting a jog without bouncing and at balancing perfectly on a lope. I could ride in the ring, I conceded. It was boring, going around and around a circle for an hour, when there was a lovely woods trail right behind the stable. But Charlotte's eyes pleaded.

"Say there, sweetheart," the man called from the front of the barn. "Come here a minute. I got something I want to show you." He was looking directly at me.

"I'm busy."

"Come on. Come up here and look in this stall. I got something good to show you. Come on, I'm not going to hurt you."

"Don't go," Charlotte breathed.

I stared at him, mesmerized by the flicker of evil behind his eyes.

"Follow me," I muttered without moving my lips. We walked up the aisle toward the man until we were even with the side door. Then we bolted.

I knocked my bike into her; our handlebars tangled. Charlotte couldn't get her kickstand up. We were on the road then, standing up on our pedals, pulling against the handlebars and rocking the bikes from side to side in our desperation for speed.

A mile away, in the safety of a gas station, we stopped to breathe, panting and sweating and staring into each other's eyes.

"This has to be a secret," I told her. "Don't tell anyone, not Carolyn or Diane, or especially your mom."

Her eyes widened. "Don't you think we should? I mean, he's probably a dangerous rapist. We should report him."

But I shook my head. The stable was too important to me. It was the stage on which I could play out my cowgirl fantasies, and those fantasies were a large part of my life. I clung to them, disappeared into them when real life frightened or bored me.

"If we tell, my folks will never let me go out to the stable again, and that would kill me, Char. That guy is only temporary, anyhow, till Bill gets back. I'm not going to tell; and if you do, I'll never have anything to do with you ever again. I won't speak to you. I won't see you even if you're standing right in front of me. You got that?"

Her eyes shifted away from mine. She didn't say anything as we pushed off and began the long uphill climb toward town, but I knew she wouldn't tell. She'd never risk losing me.

I felt my power over her, and in some twisted way it made me hate her. Because I knew she was right. I knew we should tell.

A few days later the story was on the news. A Joseph

37

Bates had been arrested for molesting a woman at his temporary place of employment, the Windsor Stable. I was forbidden to go there ever again, even though the man was safely locked up and my old friend Bill was back in charge. I begged and fumed and slammed doors, furious at Joseph Bates for robbing me of the last few months of the stable's existence, robbing me of the best part of my life that summer.

I was even furious at Charlotte because we both knew she'd been right in wanting to warn someone in authority that the man might be not quite right. After two years with her, I was accustomed to being right, always. It was hard on me to see the triumph in her eyes.

/ • /

On a hill three blocks north of the elementary school, Seventh Street ended before a pair of brick school buildings, the junior high and the high school. Behind them were the gray concrete bleachers of the field house and the fenced green rectangle of football field.

Seventh grade. The quantum leap from childhood to the big time. Our class shifted almost unbroken, up the hill and into the red brick junior high building. We'd gained and lost a few faces since fifth grade, but not many. West Des Moines was a stable little town, gradually becoming a suburb of the state capital to our east, but still a small entity by nature. Families who lived there tended to stay put.

Although I entered each school year at mental gunpoint, hating the confinement of the classroom and dreading the unknown, starting 7-B was exciting, even to me. Now we would be moving from room to room and having some choices. Art or music? There was home ec for the girls and shop for the boys; we could move around freely and make things in ovens and on turning lathes. Grimly I mastered the sewing machine and even turned out a wearable sleeveless white blouse. I never wore it, having suffered through four redoings of fitting collar to neck. But I could have; it turned out well enough in the end.

I loved the new pattern of moving from room to room rather than sitting all day in the same stifling cell. It was not impossible to sit still for fifty minutes, even through the most boring teacher's monologue. The hands on the big round clock faces jumped every minute, and I could will away fifty of those jumps easily enough.

Study halls were a gift from God. By careful management and furious cramming I always got through the work and into a library book for at least the last ten minutes or so.

Early in the year the English teacher mentioned that she had been forbidden, as a girl, to read Zane Grey's western novels. Too raw for her young eyes, she told us with a laugh. Immediately I began reading my way through all of the twenty Zane Grey books at the library, looking for the dirty parts. I was disappointed in the sex but totally absorbed by the cowboy stories.

Something in me reverberated to the fantasy in those western stories: the clear-cut good guys and bad guys, the stark beauty of desert and mountain, red earth and cactus and box canyons, flash floods crashing through arroyos. I could think of nothing in my midwestern background that should have made me that way, but there it was, a clearly defined part of my nature.

Now that I was too old for cowboy comics the Zane Grey books fed me, those and the western movies that came almost weekly to the little Lyric Theater at the far end of Main Street. By the time I was old enough to pay adult admission, I was on first-name terms with everyone at the theater. May, the huge woman in the ticket booth, jovially went on selling me the cheaper under-twelve tickets and winking as I crouched to make myself look younger. Stuart, the theater manager, sometimes let me choose among the western films when he made up his order, and regularly I was slipped a free bag of popcorn when the concessions girl cleaned the popcorn machine at nine o'clock.

By the time I climbed the hill to junior high, though, I was beginning to bury my love for western books and movies under a surface of femininity. Although I might feel I was a loner, I didn't want to be laughed at by my friends.

We were turning all our interests inward upon ourselves now, learning to decorate ourselves to please the boys. We were beginning the mating dance of the species, and I felt out of step.

I didn't want to wear a bra or any of the other awkward restrictions of womanhood. I felt right only in my jeans, and jeans were forbidden in school. Skirts and dresses for the girls, slacks for the boys. I chafed, and looked at the years stretching ahead of me. Three years of junior high, three years of senior, four years of college. It would never end.

I said that to Carolyn one day, after we'd been playing basketball in her driveway and had collapsed in the shade of the garage. It was early spring, but unseasonably hot, and we'd played a hard game.

Carolyn looked at me as though I were stupid and said, "You don't have to go to college, you know."

I stared back.

She said, "Didn't you know that?"

I shrugged. "I never thought about it. I mean, I guess I knew the dumb kids didn't go to college, but I just always figured . . . Mom and Daddy are always talking about money for putting us all through college. I never thought . . ."

But of course. You had to go to high school; only the total idiots and an occasional pregnant girl dropped out of high school. But you didn't *have* to go to college. If I didn't, it would mean glorious freedom in just five years! Something deep inside me clicked into place and the decision was made, even though I was to rethink it endlessly in high school.

Carolyn said, "Don't you want to go to college? I can hardly wait. It's going to be so much fun. Get away from home, parents, be out on your own, partying, having a ball."

"Well sure," I argued, "it's different for you. You already know that you want to be a phys ed teacher, and you have to go to college for that. But for me . . ."

"What do you really want?" For once she focused on me and listened as though she cared.

41

I shrugged and grinned. "I want to be a cowboy."

"Oh, yeah." She shoved my shoulder and grinned, and we went back to our ball game.

But things were beginning to stir in my mind.

A few nights later Charlotte and I talked. We'd walked downtown to the movie and come home slowly, stopping by the corner street sign while I made my usual attempt at climbing its three-inch-thick aluminum-painted pole. The two street signs, SIXTH STREET and ELM STREET, sat ten feet up, taunting me. Once or twice I had managed by sheer will power to climb high enough to touch ELM before slithering to the ground again.

I tried it that night, but the gripping coordination of my feet wasn't perfect and I slipped back sweaty and frustrated six times before I gave it up.

At my house we idly waited for my older sister to come home from her date, in hopes of spying on a kiss. I'd begun to be almost morbidly fascinated by any form of human coupling, from hand holding all the way to It. I wasn't entirely sure I ever wanted any of that for myself, but I was fascinated by the obvious fact that my parents had done It at least three times since they had three children.

And I was beginning to understand that all of the dressing up and lipstick and high heels and hair curling were part of an overwhelmingly large mating system that secured the survival of the species. The two sexes lined up on opposite sides, sent out signals to one another, and eventually got married and had children who

42

grew up and lined up and sent signals, and so on forever.

But I was out of it. It went on around me and over my head and had nothing to do with me. I would, of course, have to grow up and get married and do It and have babies, but the prospect depressed me.

As we sat on the front steps and waited to spy on Jeanette, I said to Charlotte, "Are you going to go to college? Did you know you don't have to if you don't want to?"

"I'm not going," she stated flatly. "I'm going to get a job like Mom's and get married. What would I want to go to college for?"

What indeed. And where would the money come from if she did want to? During the three years of our best-friendhood I had come to suspect that Charlotte's parents were divorced. She refused to talk about her father, ever, and he obviously didn't live with them. I thought that if he was dead he could be discussed. He was "away." That had been her only explanation of his absence. I was fascinated by the mystery at first, but eventually concluded that it was a genuine shame, in Charlotte's mind, and something she couldn't admit openly. So we didn't talk about it.

Her mother worked for a diaper service, running laundry machines six days a week, and money was obviously tight. It was a good thing Charlotte didn't want college. Besides, her grades wouldn't have been good enough. She played her report cards very close to the vest but it was easy to tell from classroom work that brainwise she was in the lower levels.

"I suppose you're going to college," she said with that taint of resentment that occasionally showed through her follow-the-leader attitude toward me.

I shook my head. "I don't want to. I don't know what I want to do yet, but it's going to be something more fun than four more years of studying."

She looked at me with an expression I could only describe as wonder. If I was reading her pudding face correctly, she was delighted to find that I was on her level after all.

I cringed. I wasn't on her level. I wasn't like her. I got good grades; not great ones, but pretty solid on the A and B level. Plenty good enough to go to college. If I didn't go, people would think it was because I wasn't smart enough. The Patricia Winstons of the world would assume they were better than me and would write me off as beneath their notice. The Charlottes would welcome me among them as proof that they were my equals, and they *weren't*.

Did that mean I was trapped into going to college whether I wanted it or not?

I was glad when Charlotte went home and left me to struggle with the problem.

/ • /

On a smothering, damp evening in May I walked up the hill toward school with Charlotte, Carolyn, and Diane. We wore bright new dresses and walked coltishly on high heels. Nylon hose worked against my skin with every step, making me conscious of the length of my legs. They seemed to stretch forever beneath my new skirt.

As I walked the familiar blocks, I looked at us all. We seemed pitiful to me, in some way I didn't understand. We were trying to do something here, and we were going to fail at it. Up front, Carolyn and Diane strode bumpily, their steps too long for the high-heeled shoes, so that their weight lurched at every change of stride. Small dress-up purses were awkward in our hands and threw us off our natural balance. Our hair had been crimped on metal curlers with crocodile jaws, so each upward curl ended in a down-twisted tail of hair that hadn't made it into the curler as it should have.

My own hair was already wisping against my neck and sagging over my forehead. The humidity ruined in ten minutes what had taken Jeanette all afternoon to do.

My dress was of some sheer white material like bedroom curtains, with brown piping at the edges and a small pattern of brown leaves against the white. Mom had objected to it, saying it looked more like fall than spring, but I clung to the outdoors feeling that the little leaves gave me. I had supposed that for a spring dance every young girl should wear pastel colors and flowers in her hair and all that garbage, but the flowery pink dresses I'd tried on all made me look like a caricature. The trouble with this dress was that slip straps and even bra straps showed through a little bit, and I was afraid of what the boys would say in their huddles.

Charlotte looked awful, though I don't think she

knew it. She wore a pink flowered blouse, which would have been okay for her, but below it was a wide cotton skirt of a large plaid. True, the plaid did have a few lines of pink, but mostly it was peach and coral, and it hung unevenly, too low to the ground. Her hair was gathered in a ponytail with pink plastic flowers circling it, and that would have been all right except that large wisps were already loose around the back and floating above her collar.

She walked uncomfortably close to me, as though she needed me to hold her up. As we crested the hill and tiptoed across the grass of the schoolyard to keep our heels from sinking in, she ran her hand briefly down my arm, as though seeking a handhold. I moved away slightly, to get my student activity card out of my purse. We went into the gym three abreast and brave, with Charlotte fading behind me.

It was the spring dance for the whole junior high, and it was supposed to prepare us socially for high school. We'd had three weeks of ballroom dancing lessons in the gym during the noon hour, for anyone who wanted to learn. Very few boys had come to the classes, so we'd learned with girl partners, taking turns leading. At first it had seemed easy enough; right hand out, left on partner's shoulder. Slide two steps to the right, one step back to the left. Don't look at your feet; listen to the music. I'd caught on smoothly enough until we got to the box step: I continually shifted to the other foot at the wrong time.

Dancing with other girls had been fun, but I knew the hard part was before me. Plainly and simply, I had never been that close to a male person and I was going to have to block the strangeness out of my mind long enough to remember which foot to be on. I would have to forget that I was inches away from parts of a human body I'd never seen, only in pictures in Carolyn's pamphlet about terrible diseases.

I didn't know, or care, whether my ignorance was standard for a thirteen-year-old girl. I had no brothers to exchange peeks with, and for all my hanging around in riding stables I'd never had boy companions.

A dance. Romance. Music and dreams and a kiss on the lips. That was the possibility the evening offered. We four went into the dance with our private longings dangerously close to the surface. Vulnerable.

I didn't know then what a common experience this was; school dance on a basketball floor, streamers tenting from the light fixtures and dance wax on the gleaming gold boards where on Wednesday and Friday mornings I suffered through basketball and volleyball. On bleachers along the side, teachers roosted to watch over our fun. On the edge of the stage, a three-speed record player sat wired to the loudspeaker system, dropping its stack of records methodically into place.

We sat in gray metal folding chairs near the stage and watched. Patricia Winston danced three in a row with Alton Grant. Eighth- and ninth-graders we didn't know dominated the floor. I searched the boys' faces for someone who might like my looks and come for a dance.

After a while Carolyn and Diane got up and danced with each other, laughing loudly to show how much fun they were having. Charlotte looked at me but I shook my head. It would be admitting defeat to dance with a girl.

I spotted Bruce Whiteside in a clot of boys in a far corner. By staring hard at him I thought I could send him a mental message: "Dance with Jo Herne."

He stayed safely in his corner.

Dance after dance we sat there, sometimes getting up to go to the girls' room needlessly or to shuffle through the record pile with more animation than we felt. Other girls came to sit with us for a while, and occasionally one of us would spot someone who must be talked to and hurry off. But mostly we sat.

After a while there was a Paul Jones dance. Everybody on the floor, form two circles, girls in the center, boys on the outside. At last! We ran to join hands in the inner circle, looking outward into the faces of the elusive boys. The music began and we circled right while the boy-line skimmed past in the opposite direction. The music stopped and everybody grabbed.

But there weren't enough boys to go around, and I didn't grab fast enough. Red-faced, I eased back to my chair and waited it out.

Later, when I was beginning to sneak peeks at my watch to see whether it was time to cut the fun and leave, I looked up to find a boy actually standing in front of me, grinning down and holding out his hand.

Roberto.

Not my romance, not a hope for a future boyfriend, just my smiling friend Roberto. I followed him to the floor and into the music. At that point I didn't care if I was crossing social lines, I was merely, overwhelmingly glad he'd broken my losing streak for me.

He held me lightly but firmly against his rounded front and kept his feet away from my sliding, stiff two-step. We didn't try to talk, needing all our concentration for our feet, but he grinned throughout the dance and gave me a cheering squeeze of the hand when it was over.

"Thank you," he said sweetly, and I blurted, "No, thank *you*. I didn't think I was ever going to get off that darn chair."

I watched him after that, hoping he'd come back, but he seemed to be methodically dancing with every girl in our class. He danced several times with Mary, who was his natural mate, and with her he relaxed and talked and laughed and jitterbugged. With the rest of us he seemed to be extending a courtesy.

Toward the end of the evening there was a ladies' choice. Hot dog! I thought, propelled from my chair by the urgency of quick action. Bruce Whiteside was far away behind a corner of the bleachers. I got to him two lengths in front of another girl and asked him.

He looked dismayed, but we made it onto the floor and into each other's arms. He was half a head shorter than I, and his narrow hand felt ice cold and trembly in mine. Why I still felt an affinity for this quiet little guy after all this time I wasn't sure. He was bright, he was clean, he was somehow superior in a way that the bolder boys were not. He was mine, even if he didn't know it yet.

When the music ended he walked me back to my chair, which proved that he knew where I'd been all evening. New music was starting and I held my breath, but he thanked me and sat me down and disappeared behind the bleachers again. It was the last I saw of him all night.

At eleven o'clock the four of us walked down the hill in the same formation we'd climbed it three hours earlier. Our hair straggled in the damp night air, and our dresses clung to our backs as though sweaty hands still pressed them.

"That was fun," Charlotte said bravely.

The rest of us grunted.

"That stupid Dale," Diane said with sudden venom. "How come you kept dancing with him, anyway?" Jealousy rang unmistakably in her voice.

"Because he's a boy, and he asked me," Carolyn said reasonably. "You know who didn't come? Hazel Stott. I wonder why she didn't come."

Charlotte snorted. "With a face like that? Heck, we hardly got asked to dance all evening, and we're ten times better looking than Hazel Stott. She wouldn't have the nerve to come."

I felt a twist of discomfort, thinking about Hazel. It would be awful to be so ugly you didn't come to school dances.

And yet, I admitted after a block of silent walking, she might have been smarter than I, after all. I'd danced one dance with a boy too timid to escape me and one other with a boy too kind-hearted to leave girls sitting alone all evening. I'd built up a headful of unrealistic, romantic hopes for the evening, and when they died they hung like a weight around my neck. I could have stayed home and read a book and had a happier Friday night.

Which of us was on the right track, I wondered, Hazel Stott or me?

Ninth grade. My last year in junior high. It occurred to me as I walked into my assigned home room on that first morning that it was four years since the day I'd been the new kid in class and Mr. Lane had drawn me a horse on the blackboard. And here I was, still not entirely assimilated into the group. Here I was, still without the genuine best friend I needed.

The faces I passed on my way to a window seat were so familiar they hardly needed greeting: Patricia and her friends; Bruce Whiteside sitting near the front as he always did, eager to see and hear and learn; Hazel by the far wall, working at being invisible; Mary and Roberto in the center, where they could pass notes in all directions.

And a new face.

She sat one desk ahead of me and in the next row,

where I could look her over carefully without being seen. I liked her. The more I looked, the more I liked. She had tan skin and hair almost the same color, a lithe, athletic body designed for jeans and saddles, and clear, gray-green eyes that surveyed this room full of strangers with fearless intelligence.

Ahh, I thought. This one is it. This one is mine. Finally, a friend of the mind.

The girl had clear-cut features a little too sharp to be pretty, and she wore no makeup at all, not even lipstick. The style suited her. She looked scoured by a desert wind. Even her hair was just right, boyishly short and waving naturally back in a curve around her ears. The hairstyle was a mark of courage in a time when everyone I knew, myself included, wore hair parted on the side, combed straight down, curled up at the bottom.

Mrs. Mahoney called us to order at the ringing of the bell and introduced the three new students, two boys I hadn't noticed, and Pam Underwood, who had transferred to Valley from Roosevelt High in Des Moines.

I didn't like the sound of that. I wanted her to have come from some small town far away from Des Moines, or better yet from Colorado. She looked like open air and mountains. I didn't want her to be from Roosevelt, the most socially elite high school in Des Moines. That could set her dangerously close to Patricia's circle.

Our first class of the day was biology. I'd taken it because it was one of the tougher classes offered, and I needed to separate myself from Charlotte's level. Also, I was curious to see the insides of animals.

53

Pam was in the class, too. I fell into step beside her and said, "Hi. I'm Jo Herne. Welcome to Valley." I wanted to say more, but shyness, and the need to make a good first impression fast, tangled my tongue.

She smiled and said, "Hi. Thanks."

"This must seem pretty small compared to Roosevelt."

She grinned widely and nodded, and we went into the science room together.

The teacher was Mr. Funkhouser, whose name was in constant danger on the lips of ninth-graders. He was young and trim and was, in fact, the basketball coach; he taught two science classes because his contract forced him to, not because he had any interest in anything but basketball. Carolyn signed up for biology because she knew she could get a good grade from Funkhouser without opening a book all year. All she had to do was to go on being top-scoring forward on the freshman team, and she had every intention of doing that.

Mr. Funkhouser wrote his name on the blackboard, then did the standard welcoming speech. "Now, class, we are here to study the anatomy of living things, and we can best do that by opening them up and looking inside. Some of you may be a little squeamish at first, but you'll get over it. I know that many of you are considering professions in medicine, so this class will be of utmost importance in learning the basics of animal life, including the human animal."

Roberto did a low tiger growl. I turned and grinned at him. I hadn't seen him come into the class and was a little surprised to find him there. Biology was, after all, one of the brain classes. And Roberto was neither a brain nor an athlete. Far from it. Carolyn and three tall boys in the back were in the class for obvious reasons having more to do with making the basketball team than with medical careers. But Roberto certainly wasn't here to make points with the basketball coach. Oh, well.

Mr. Funkhouser went on. "You'll find that there is little time wasted in this class, students. We will begin our first dissections tomorrow, starting with the earthworm."

Shuffling, giggling, gagging sounds rippled through the class.

"Since our budget doesn't allow for worms for everyone, we will divide into teams of two, and we'll keep those teams throughout the semester, from earthworms all the way through frogs. Now, I have no objection to friends working together, so long as the work gets done. If you have a preference for a team partner, let's see hands."

Instantly I waved and pointed at Pam Underwood's head. But I wasn't the only one.

Mr. Funkhouser began to write, glancing at us. "Okay, that will be, let's see," he named off the pairs. "Carter and Huff, Winston and Underwood, Herne and . . . let's see, who do we have left? Herne and Stott. And Rodriguez, you're left over. You'll have to have a worm all to yourself."

I turned to catch Roberto's pantomime of dropping a worm into his mouth. If anyone had to be left over without a partner, Roberto was best. His feelings wouldn't be hurt, as mine would have been if I'd been odd man out. Roberto could make a joke of anything.

Then my eyes met Hazel's. My lab partner for the whole semester, worms through frogs. Her small eyes glowed with an emotion I couldn't read. It looked almost like hate, for an instant. Then her oatmeal skin reddened as though she'd given away an intimacy, and she looked down at her biology book.

I took the biology pairing as an unimportant setback in my courting of Pam Underwood. I listened when she talked in class, and found her to be bright, confident, and funny. Her mind worked at the same speed as mine, and the same things struck us as funny. Together we were the first to laugh when Roberto, doing an anatomically impossible take-off on Abe Lincoln, raised his finger in the air and proclaimed, "There is strength in the onion!"

"That's *union*, Roberto," the teacher corrected him. Pam's eyes met mine and we laughed together.

On Friday afternoon I managed to catch Pam at her locker and said, "Say, a bunch of us are going into town tonight, roller skating, Charlotte Yoder and Carolyn and Diane and I. Want to come?" I held my breath.

She looked mildly surprised. "Oh, I can't. I've got a date. But thanks anyway."

"Oh. Yeah, well, some other time, then."

"Sure."

I backed away, humiliated. She had been in this school exactly five days, and she had a date already. I'd been here four years and I was nowhere near a date.

And now she knew I spent my Friday nights roller skating with Charlotte Yoder.

I watched from the partial shelter of my locker as she walked out the door with Patricia Winston, and I knew that was the end of it.

Late in the school year our class was given a day of special tests that had nothing to do with the subjects we were studying. Part of the test was designed to help us choose careers, to separate the college-bound from the dumber ones. The other half of the test was IQ, to give a specific ranking to us according to brains.

I found the tests fun. The first set asked questions such as "Would you rather cook a meal or dig a hole?" There were no right or wrong answers, only preferences. The second part was like puzzles or word games, and I'd always been a whiz at those.

Two days later we had individual conferences with our home room teachers about our test results. Mrs. Mahoney called me to the chair beside her desk and sat staring down at my test results and breathing loudly through her nose with a tiny whistling sound.

"So?" I said. "How did I do?"

"Well, Joanne, on the first test your scores are a little mixed."

"Uh-oh."

"No, there's nothing wrong, I didn't mean that. It's just that you don't seem to fit into any of our categories."

I laughed. I could have told her that.

"You're certainly bright enough for a college-bound," she said slowly, "but your scores on the preference tests put you into"—she frowned—"farming as a career choice. Well, I expect that means you'd better marry a farmer." She smiled and looked relieved, having finally gotten me into a category.

"*Marry* a farmer? Why can't I *be* a farmer? Why do I have to marry it instead of being it?"

"Well, but you're a girl, dear." She actually patted my arm.

I steamed.

She went on. "Now, on the IQ portion of the test you did amazingly well." She glanced at me uncertainly, as though I might be someone else in disguise. "If these test scores are correct," she said dubiously, "you would rank in the top two percentile, nationally."

I let that sink in. "You mean I'm smarter than ninety-eight percent of kids my age?"

"Well, dear, we can't take these test scores too seriously now, can we?"

"Why not, if I earned it?"

She lowered her chin and looked at me over her glasses. "Your grades don't reflect it, Joanne. You should be a straight-A student."

I let that go by. I simply didn't care enough about the subjects we studied, nor did I care enough about competitive achievement against my classmates. My struggle was to find my place among them or to learn to live comfortably without them.

"Did I get the highest score in the class?" I asked.

"Second highest."

Second highest. That raised an obvious question. "Who was highest?"

She hesitated, then decided to trust me with the information. "Bruce Whiteside."

I grinned and glowed. The two of us, Bruce and I, at the top of the class. Fervently I hoped he knew I was up there with him.

As I got up from my chair another question occurred. "Who was third?" I wanted it not to be Patricia or any of her friends, and I wanted it not to be Pam Underwood. Since she had chosen Patricia instead of me, I needed a clear superiority over all of them.

Mrs. Mahoney smiled with sudden warmth and said, "Hazel Stott."

/ • /

Three fat, yellow school buses rolled down the highway on a bright May morning. The entire ninth grade, complete with teacher-chaperones, was headed south, to Lake Ahquabi, for the junior-high equivalent of Senior Skip Day. The day was our farewell gift from Valley Junior High, and the best part was that it was a weekday and the rest of the school was in class, working as usual.

I was in the second bus, with the rest of 9-B. Of course, Charlotte sat next to me in the window seat. Carolyn was behind us, but not with Diane. Dale Ellert had maneuvered in beside her, and Charlotte spent most of the trip trying to watch them without moving her head. By the time we were ten miles down the road I was ready to rip off her arm and beat her with it the next time she nudged me with her fat elbow to call my attention to Carolyn and Dale.

It was bound to happen, I thought dismally. We couldn't all stay boyfriendless forever, and we were practically sophomores. Carolyn was nice-looking enough, and Dale was the star center on the junior high boys' team, with sure prospects for stardom in senior high. What could be more natural than for him and Carolyn to hook onto each other?

It irritated me that she'd done it in secret, though. I'd confided in her about Bruce Whiteside, and she'd never said one word about liking Dale. And here they were sitting together on the class trip, which was a pretty public statement.

Okay for her, I thought bitterly.

I leaned forward and donged Mary's ponytail and said, "Hey, Mare, let's get some singing started. What's a bus trip without singing?"

Her black eyes gleamed at me. Such a pretty girl. Such a carefree, confident, enviable girl. I couldn't hate her, because she was so thoroughly nice, but I would have if I could.

She bounced up and stood in the aisle, facing backward toward the group, her hands braced on seat backs.

"No standing in the aisle," the driver bellowed good-naturedly. Mary squatted and sat on the out-bent knee of Mrs. Mahoney, who was wearing slacks just like a regular person that day. Balanced thus, Mary raised her hands and pulled a long face, and said in the twang of our rather peculiar Glee Club leader, "All right now, young folks, we can't sing if we aren't orderly."

It was an unmistakable takeoff on Mr. Webber, and I

saw Mrs. Mahoney's face stiffen momentarily, then relax.

Mary directed us to attention with her hands and said in Webber's voice, "Attention now, young folks. We are going to sing our school song. Ready? *One*-and-a, *two*-and-a . . . Beer, beer for old Valley High, pour out the bourbon, bring on the rye . . ."

We bellowed along with her:

> "Send a freshman out for gin,
> Don't let a sober person in.
> We never stagger, never fall,
> We sober up on wood alcohol,
> While our loyal sons are marching
> Back to the bar for more.
> Tra la la la la la . . ."

Most of us in that bus had never tasted liquor, but we loved our version of the school fight song. It made us feel wise and wicked.

From Roberto in the back of the bus came the next song. "R.A.G.G., M.O.P.P., rag-mop, rag-mop, doodle-ee-oo . . ." He swung his curly head and tromped his feet on the floor and flapped his hands.

Just looking at Roberto still made me smile, but sometimes now his clowning irritated me. It seemed such an act, and it was so constant. He could be sitting quietly reading, I'd say hi to him in passing, and instantly the comedy act started. "How high?" was his usual reply. Then he'd start singing, "How high the moon."

I'd like to have tried a serious conversation with him sometime. I'd like to have known what his life was like, and his dreams for his future. There seemed to be something more than a D-student clown behind that smooth round face, but I couldn't get through to it.

I couldn't get through to Bruce Whiteside, either. He sat well behind me with the boys and managed never to meet my glance. Generally the boys had the back of the bus and the girls the front, but in between were a few seats holding couples: Carolyn and Dale, Patricia Winston and Alton Grant, and two other upper-level couples. Maybe dating starts at the top and filters down, I thought. But if so, Carolyn was a traitor to her group.

We got to the lake by ten and poured out of the buses, whooping. It was a small blue lake set in rolling green lawns broken by stretches of pine woods. Heavy timbers lined the parking area and the paths. The swimming beach was a clean, raked expanse of fine sand, and we had it all to ourselves.

Charlotte tried to drag me into the women's changing room with her, but I'd worn my swimsuit under my jeans on the bus. I shook her off and ran free of her, to pile my jeans and blouse and penny loafers at the rim of the beach and run into the water.

I wasn't a good swimmer, having had few chances to learn, but I relished the feel of silky water sliding over my skin and the silence of holding my head under water. I loved feeling my hair rise away from my scalp to float like seaweed.

Pam Underwood came in close behind me and swam past me with actual swimming strokes. She paused to tread water and we smiled at each other. Then she side-stroked over to a pair of boys, and they welcomed her. I couldn't have done that. I couldn't have approached boys. She just calmly assumed they'd want her company, and they did. I turned away and held my nose and sank until I was alone and my hair was seaweed.

Somehow I had come to the point of thinking that boys had ceased to belong to my race. They'd assumed an importance that set them on their own rarefied plane and made them impossible to approach naturally. In some unfathomable way, the least of them had become more valuable than the best of the girls.

Friendships among girls might be desired or taken for granted or undesired, but they were essentially unimportant. I'd spent years now wishing for someone better than Charlotte to hang around with but not caring enough to do much about it. I'd never pursued a girl's friendship except for my one sad attempt at Pam Underwood's. I'd never felt a strong need for one. A friend, yes, someone to tell things to and feel close to. But not a girlfriend as such. It was a fine distinction, but a clear one. I didn't enjoy flocking with the crowd for shopping trips to Des Moines. I preferred seeing movies alone so I could get lost in the story. I didn't *want* to be one of the ewe flock.

But a boyfriend was entirely different. By now, at fourteen, it was clear to me that girls were graded according to their ability to get boyfriends. And obviously I flunked.

And I didn't understand why.

And it made me want to bawl.

I knew that my looks were somewhere in the middle range. Not pretty, not ugly. My hair was ordinary brown; I wore it in the same style as most of the others, although I was continually tempted to whack it off short like Pam's. My shape was rather angular, with shoulders too wide and square for the thinness below them, but I had a decent set of female equipment.

I was smart. The seventh-grade IQ tests were my proof of that. I was pleasant. I lent books to any boy who asked, and I tried to kid around with them although it usually came out sounding stiff and false.

Obviously there was something wrong with me that I didn't know about. The boys knew about it. Bruce knew about it and avoided me even though he was the right and logical one to be my boyfriend through our high school years.

I'd read somewhere that our own voices never sound the same to us as they do to other people; they echo through our sinus passages or something. So, I reasoned, maybe we look different to ourselves than we look to everyone else. Maybe we don't see our flaws, just as we don't hear our voices truly or smell our own body odor.

Probably that was it, I decided. Probably I'm uglier than I realize. Probably that's why Charlotte has always assumed that I was on her level or that she was on mine.

I came out of the water and walked deliberately up to Hazel Stott and studied her. She hadn't gone in swimming and instead was helping the teachers get the lunch ready, setting out paper plates and jars of relish and mustard.

She caught my eye and looked away without smiling. Her hands trembled as she tore at a potato chip bag, trying to open it.

Just then I wanted to talk to her as I'd sometimes wanted to talk to Roberto. I wanted to understand what she felt and thought and dreamed about, behind her homely face. Her solitude was so much thicker than mine. Did she really want it that way?

But I turned away from her and went to stand beside the barbecue, stabbing at wieners. I'd needed Hazel just then because she made me feel better about my own ugliness, and I was ashamed to have done that to her in my mind.

After lunch we all lay around on the sloping grass digesting, flirting, dozing. A little way down the beach was a small, rotting dock where rowboats could be rented for three dollars an hour. Patricia and Alton rowed away, then several others in sets of two, Mary and Roberto, Carolyn and Dale, pairs of whooping boys and other pairs of yelling, splashing girls.

"Come on." Charlotte dragged at my arm. "I've got two dollars. Have you got any money? Come on, let's get a boat."

"Go with somebody else for a change. Take Hazel." I hadn't meant to sound so snippy. She stared at me, startled and wounded. I'd hurt her not only by wanting to be rid of her but by classifying her with Hazel. I hadn't meant to do that. I'd been feeling vaguely sorry for

Hazel, that was all, and sorry for myself for enduring Charlotte's endless small demands.

Her pancake face hardened against me, and she turned and stalked off toward the boat dock. A few minutes later she rowed away with a girl I knew only by name, a rather fat girl.

Relieved and depressed, I pulled my jeans and blouse on over my damp swimsuit, shoved into my loafers, and strode away up a bark path into the woods.

Ah. This was what I wanted. The woods were like an underwater world, the air tinted green from sunlight picking its way through oak leaves and pine boughs. Ferns grew thick beside the path and, in a sunny spot, tiny wild strawberries glowed like a scattering of rubies in the grass. I picked a few and sucked the tartness out of them and walked on.

It was a relief, a blessing, when childhood fantasies began to play through my head. I was riding up the trail on my good stallion, winding upward through the mountains toward my peaceful home in the valley beyond the next saddleback. I lived alone in my mountain valley, in a little log cabin full of books and firewood. I didn't have to mess with anybody, and nobody messed with me.

Whether I was male or female in this dream was unclear, unimportant. I was a person. Myself. Solitary and sufficient.

I stayed in the woods as long as I dared, following divergent paths and circling reluctantly back toward the beach at four o'clock, when we were scheduled to leave.

Clots of wet-haired swimmers stood near the buses, waiting.

When Charlotte came over to me to show me her truly impressive rowing blisters, I admired them and the truce was sealed.

"What are we waiting for?" a voice called.

"Nose count," another answered. "We're not all here yet. Who's missing? Who's missing?"

Teachers and bus drivers began sorting through us, matching people with lists of names.

"Patricia Winston."

"Alton Grant."

Aha. We looked at one another, sensing drama. Patricia and Alton had been in the first rowboat to go out, almost three hours before. We moved toward the lake and shaded our eyes and stared into the glare on the water, looking for the boat.

Worried looks shot between adults. A drowning tragedy. A double drowning. And they'd be blamed. The search was organized somehow, two boats going left around the lake, two going right. Stay close to the shore, be careful, yell if you find them. Someone was sent to the park office to notify the ranger. The rest of us were commanded to stay in or near the buses and not wander off.

We sat in quiet groups, subdued and tensed by the idea of death. Charlotte held my hand and I let her for a while. Glancing around, I saw other hands clasped. Even the boys seemed to stand or lean close to each other.

67

Forty minutes later the boats came back, five of them. Strong voices called to us, "We found them. They're okay. No sweat."

Patricia and Alton walked toward us, both glowing deep crimson, both averting their eyes from ours. Charlotte and I raised eyebrows at each other.

We climbed into the B bus and took seats similar to our earlier ones, except that Alton sat in the middle of the long back seat, side-poking and whispering with his friends, and Patricia rode with Mrs. Mahoney.

The whisper reached us from behind. Carolyn leaned forward and drew our heads down close to hers at the crack between the seat backs. "Patricia and Alton got caught."

"Doing what?" Charlotte whispered back.

"*It,* stupid. They were doing *It.* In a rowboat. Can you imagine? Mr. Evans and Mr. Dean rowed right up beside them and caught them actually doing It! They'll probably get kicked out of school."

I was awed. Fifteen years old and Patricia Winston already knew the secrets and the mysteries. She might even be going to have a baby. She might have to drop out of school. I felt a surge of triumph over her.

Leaning forward and donging Mary's ponytail, I passed on the delicious news. Mary looked not at me but forward, toward Patricia. "Oh, poor Pat," she breathed. "This must be the worst moment of her life."

I sank back in my seat, defeated by a goodness that towered above my own.

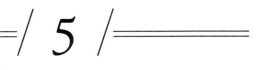

The car door slammed shut, enclosing me in a moving capsule of gaiety. This was our breakthrough night! I twisted around to look at Charlotte in the driver's seat and Carolyn and Diane in the back. Spontaneously we lifted our fists and cheered.

Our first night out together on our own. It was mid-July, before our junior year. Charlotte had just passed her sixteenth birthday and had, only that afternoon, been issued a full-fledged driver's license. The rest of us were months away from ours, but all we needed was one—one driver's license and a parent willing to trust us with a car.

We'd taken a rough vote the day before and decided to celebrate the big night in three stages: first, the roller rink, then our first attempt to scoop the loop, and finally a slumber party at my house. The trunk of

Charlotte's mother's Ford was crammed with sleeping bags and paper sacks of night things.

I noticed immediately that I was the only one wearing jeans. We had always worn jeans to the skating rink when we were younger. It was only recently that Charlotte, then Diane, and finally Carolyn had begun wearing full-circle skirts. They weren't going for the skating anymore, only for the hunting.

Charlotte drove in a jerky, self-conscious way; to cover her inexperience, she went somewhat faster than she should have. I sat sideways and kept my eyes on Carolyn and Diane so I wouldn't have to see where we were going. It was a safe enough drive, really, along Grand Avenue, past the disappearing open fields that separated city from suburb, past the Art Center and the mansions, and down a long hill into the center of the city.

It was Friday night, and the rink was full. High in the vaulted ceiling, large fans dispersed body heat and July dampness and the worst of the racket. Along one side of the rink, large, glassless windows opened to a view of the Des Moines River beyond the trees of Waterworks Park. The faint smell of river water and fish came to me as I coasted along.

At one end, on a high platform, sat an organist playing the music that measured our glides. Around the outer edge of the golden, oval floor, the nervous beginners teetered and reached for the battered plank wall. The medium-proficient stroked along in the middle areas, while the serious skaters, perfecting spins, practiced with blank-faced intensity in the center.

70

As soon as my wheels were on the rink I stroked away from Charlotte and the others, hungering for speed, dodging the slower bodies in front of me, crossing over with my outside foot on the turns. The crowds frustrated me. I wanted to skate backward, fast, lacing my strides and swinging my arms, but there was no room.

When the music ended, the organist said into his mike, "Next number, couples only. Couples only, please."

Growling to myself, I began to coast toward the side, but before I hit the sideboards, hands gripped me around the waist. Masculine hands. The music started, "The Tennessee Waltz," and I was part of it.

At first I didn't look at him, I was too busy getting into step with his legs, feeling the diagonal support of his arm across my back. He took my left hand in his, pulling it across his body so that my shoulder nestled securely under his. It felt wonderful!

When my balance was firm enough, I glanced at his face. It was round and red, with pale hair cropped short above his ears, and brows and lashes nearly white. His lips were thick, his smile bland. The fingers that rested on my hip, beneath my right hand, were red and blunt and sausagelike.

After a few rounds he spun me in front of him and we skated face to face, arms twined, faces close. I traveled backward effortlessly, powered and guided by him. Charlotte skated by with a rather fat boy I'd never seen. Carolyn and Diane watched from the sidelines. They no longer skated or danced together; Carolyn didn't like to.

71

When the waltz ended, my boy offered a Coke and we settled at one of the tiny tables near the refreshment counter. I was nerved up with the necessity of making a good enough impression in the next few minutes to keep him with me for the evening. Chances like this came to me so seldom.

Bucky, he said his name was. I didn't catch the last name because it was tricky and the noise level was impossible, and I didn't want to ask him to say it more than once. Bucky. I liked that.

"Jo Herne," I yelled. I don't think he got the last name, either. "Where do you go?"

"Clive," he said.

I nodded and gave him my school. Clive was a small rural high school not far from my old riding stable. "Do you live on a farm?" I asked, thinking it would be fun to date a farmer. He might have a horse, we could go riding, have romantic moments in the barn . . .

His round face became suddenly defensive. "Yeah. I farm. So what?"

I looked puzzled. "So nothing. Why do you say it like that?"

He sniffed and sucked his Coke. "You're a town girl, I suppose." It sounded faintly like an insult.

I bridled. "Yes, I live in town, if you call West Des Moines a town. Why? What difference does it make?"

He wrinkled his thick upper lip and shrugged. "What year you in?"

I looked at him for a second before I answered. "I'll be a sophomore. What difference does it make if I'm a town girl or not? I love the country. I love horses. I used to go riding all the time at Windsor Stable before it closed. I can't help it if I live in town. I wouldn't, if it were up to me."

He shrugged again, and I could feel him withdrawing. He glanced back at the rink.

"Look," I said with some desperation, "why did you ask me to skate? I mean, did you like the way I look, or was I the only one handy, or what?"

Again the shrug, the averted eyes. "You were in front of me when the music started," he said.

"Oh, that's wonderful. That makes me feel terrific." I warmed my voice with a note of laughter, and he responded with a half-smile.

"And you weren't all dressed up," he said.

I pondered that. "Aha. I was wearing jeans, so you thought maybe I wasn't a town girl, since you seem to have a grudge against anyone who doesn't live on a farm; am I right so far? You apparently have some kind of inferiority complex and you're afraid a town girl might look down on you for being a farmer, right?"

He seemed confused. It occurred to me that I was thinking circles around the poor jerk. What was I doing wasting my time and energy trying to impress somebody who wasn't good enough for me?

I sucked up the last of my Coke and stood teetering on my wheels. "Thank you very much for the Coke, Bucky. See you around." I clopped off through the crowd and glided onto the rink in blessed solitude.

A little later I saw a familiar form coasting along ahead of me at half my speed. With a daring flare I spun in front of him and held up my arms. Roberto's round brown face lit with a jack-o'-lantern grin as he put his hands on my shoulders and received my weight. I hooked my hands over his biceps, threw my head back, and relaxed in the support and enjoyment of good old Roberto.

"Who'd you come with?" he asked after a while.

"Charlotte and a bunch. You?"

"Couple of the guys."

We skated silently for half a round. Then I said, "You don't date anybody special, do you, Roberto?" It was more statement than question.

He laughed and said, "Nah, I've got so many after me, it's just too much trouble picking out one."

I nodded. "Yeah, I have that problem too."

We skated on in silent enjoyment and stayed together for the next couples-only waltz. He was a pleasure to skate with, a slow, easy pleasure that didn't demand fancy kick steps like some of the couples were doing, or even conversation. He was warm and soft and steady to lean into. When Bucky sailed past with another blue-jeaned girl I gave him a cool look.

As we skated I thought, what if he asks me out? What if he wants to take me someplace after skating? I couldn't tonight, because of the slumber party at my house, but what if he asks me for some other time?

I'd have to make an excuse. Much as I liked Roberto and enjoyed his company, I couldn't go out on a date with him. We would both be snickered about at school. She couldn't get an American guy, so she went with Roberto Rodriguez; he couldn't get any of the Mexican girls, so he went with Jo Herne. We'd both be diminished by a crossing of the line.

And still, I wanted him to ask. But when Charlotte waved me over to the side at ten-thirty and said they were ready to leave, Roberto handed me over with no sign of regret and rejoined his friends. I was left to wonder whether he was as afraid of jumping the line as I was or whether he was simply disinterested, just being kind again to the wallflower.

"Now to scoop the loop," Carolyn said with satisfaction as we settled into the Ford. "Ya-a-y," we cheered.

Excitement brightened our eyes as we swung onto Locust Street and began the mating dance of our species, of our time. Charlotte drove slowly from stop light to stop light so that we could search out responsive faces in the cars on either side of us. Past block after block of downtown Des Moines we coasted with the one-way flow toward the river and the golden dome of the capitol building beyond. Then, back again on Walnut Street past Sears and Penney's and Younkers Department Store where our school clothes came from, north again onto Locust, and around once more.

There were cars full of boys hunting as we were. They called to us at red lights, leered at us or asked what school we went to, did we know so-and-so, what year were we. Some cars had only one or two boys; with those we exchanged looks, maybe smiles, then passed them by.

Midway in our second circuit a pink-and-gray Chevy loaded with chrome zeroed in on us and stopped beside us at a yellow light we both could have driven through if we'd wanted to. There were four boys inside, one for each of us. But when we saw their faces more closely, Carolyn slid low in the backseat and whispered, "Let's peel out of here. They're creeps."

The hair was long and dirty looking, skin and teeth looked bad, and their faces leered at us through the windows in a way that reminded me of the man at the riding stable.

"Turn left up here," I said under my breath.

Charlotte did a fast and dangerous left turn from the center lane and we cheered ourselves for having lost them.

"Let's go around one more time," Charlotte said.

"Nah," Diane muttered from the backseat, "this is boring. Let's go on home."

We'd just made the turn onto Grand Avenue when the pink-and-gray Chevy appeared behind us, honking and sprouting waving arms.

A look of uneasiness bordering on fear passed across Charlotte's face.

"Just keep driving," I told her. "As long as we keep moving they can't do anything to us."

Diane crouched in the backseat to watch our followers through the rear window. Carolyn stuck her arm out her window and sent them a graphic message, an obscene gesture that I didn't realize she knew.

The Chevy followed us all the way to West Des Moines, then drifted away in the direction of the bowling alley.

"Whew," we said in chorus.

"That could have been dangerous, you know," I said, and they agreed.

Oh, but it was exciting.

Hours later I lay awake, staring at nothing, but unable to slow my thoughts down to sleep speed. Charlotte lay beside me, her backbone modestly turned in my direction. On the floor Carolyn and Diane lay, carefully separate, with their sleeping bags under them for softness.

There was an ache chewing at me. It was a soft and melancholy hunger for something that the evening had brought out but not quite identified. It had to do with Bucky sheering off of me when I began to talk, when I began to reason above the level of his intelligence. It had to do with Roberto's warm hands that willingly gave me back to my friends when I didn't want to be given back!

It had to do with cars full of young people driving in mindless circles through the night streets, trying to find one another, trying to make a contact that would lead somehow to being loved.

It had to do with these three people who shared my bedroom and were nothing more to me than an intrusion in my essential loneliness.

/ • /

Once again our class moved intact to another building, this time to the high school building next door to our familiar old junior high. We were now Valley Tigers and Tigerettes.

At least *they* were. School spirit seemed faintly ridiculous to me. High school was a three-year period of our lives that we happened to be passing through on our way to the real world.

As far as I could tell, I was the only one in 10-B who felt that way. Charlotte joined Glee Club and Pep Club; Mary Valdez leaped into cheerleading and made the squad in tenth grade, a rare accomplishment. Bruce Whiteside grew four inches and went out for the debating team. I was in the audience at every debate and was continually surprised at the quality of his thinking and the smoothness of his arguments.

Carolyn, of course, made the varsity basketball team and played in every game her first year. I was proud of her in a detached way. Charlotte made the most of reflected glory, and Diane glowered possessively from the bleachers. By Christmastime Carolyn and Dale had exchanged letter sweaters, and she ceased to be a friend to do things with.

Patricia and Alton Grant were going steady, too, apparently undamaged by their rowboat disaster.

I was filled with a sense of suspension, treading water until I was freed to swim away into the ocean or ride off into the mountains. I seemed unnatural to myself, but apparently it didn't show to the people around me. I was accepted well enough, even by the boys in my classes; but for reasons I couldn't understand, no one came close.

When the football season started, Charlotte and I walked to the games together, but she sat in the Pep Club section, where everyone wore orange school sweaters and, on signals from the cheerleaders, held up cardboard squares that spelled "Go Tigers."

I sat high up on the top row of bleachers, usually alone, and pretended I was on a mountaintop looking out over a wooded valley instead of a Valley ball game. I watched the time clock instead of the game and sighed impatiently through every time-out. Boys walked past beneath me and sometimes threw me a "hi," but they never came to sit with me.

Of course, I could have joined Pep Club if I'd wanted to. It was hardly an exclusive group, since nearly half of the student body belonged. Obeying instincts I barely understood, I veered away from joining groups just to be joining.

The same was true of Glee Club. I loved singing to myself, especially western ballads or country-western heart wringers, but standing in tiers with sixty other kids in white blouses, singing obscure choral pieces no one had ever heard of, wasn't for me.

By the end of my sophomore year I found myself more alone than I had ever been within a school. Occasionally my attention would be caught by a new girl or one I hadn't considered before, and I'd think about asking her over after school. But I didn't want to go through another Pam Underwood experience. I felt breakable beneath my calm exterior.

Although Charlotte and I were still best friends, it was a friendship in name only. We seldom did things together in the evenings, and the phone conversations dwindled. She was finding other friends, other herd members. After years of irritation at having to play oak to her clinging-ivy act, it was astonishing how bereft I felt.

/ • /

The summer after tenth grade we took a family vacation for the first time. Jeanette had married a Valley boy after graduation, and they were living in Denver that summer, where he was stationed in the air force. We were to deliver a trunkload of her belongings and do some sight-seeing along the way.

For the past few years I'd been shrinking away from my family. They irritated me simply by existing so close to me, and I irritated them. I needed space and solitude, and sometimes I clawed my way clear of them with a shrill voice and touchy temperament. I liked myself no better than they did when the outbursts happened, and yet I knew deep down that I was all right. This was not the real me. It was as temporary as high school and would correct itself when my outward life could finally be fitted to my needs.

The prospect of ten days cooped up in the car with the three of them would have been unbearable except for our destination. The actual, genuine West!

We started very early on a July morning and drove with only necessary stops north and west across Iowa, then straight across interminable South Dakota. Then suddenly we were in the *West*: the Badlands, with fantastic red rock formations; Deadwood, a tourists' frontier town with rough plank buildings and taverns with swinging doors. There were dramatic reenactments of the shooting of Wild Bill Hickok, carnival rides, and horse-drawn stagecoaches. I had my picture taken on a stuffed bucking bronc, my arm raised dramatically over my head.

Then we circled south through Wyoming and into the Rocky Mountains. At last. There were the Rattlesnake Hills, and Cheyenne and Laramie igniting my imagination. My nose never left the car window. We were driving through a painting, a movie set. No, this was real.

I went quietly nuts.

The visit with Jeanette meant nothing to me. I spent my time staring out the window of her air force bungalow at the hazy blue-green mountains behind the city.

The three-day drive home was an endless imprisonment with Judy taking up more than her share of the backseat, Mom up front having headaches, and Daddy silent and surly whenever bathroom stops were asked for. I disappeared into my own head and rode with my eyes closed.

/ 6 /

On a snowy Saturday night in January of my senior year, I sat in the projection booth at the Lyric Theater and looked down at my friends. For two years now I'd worked behind the candy counter three nights a week, and the place had become a warm center in my life. Often on nights when I wasn't working, like tonight, I came down anyway and sat in the back of the theater or up in the projection booth, where I was always welcomed and given the catbird seat.

The catbird seat was a battered old theater seat mounted on a low platform and set sideways to the wall, just behind a window that looked down onto the theater and the screen. To the right of the seat were the twin projection machines, head-high and horse-long, that aimed their animated cones of light through small trap doors, through the smoky air of the theater, and onto the screen. They worked one at a time, so that the next reel of film could be threaded into one machine while the movie was progressing on the other.

Each reel was twenty minutes long, and about a minute before the end of the reel, a small circle would flash in the upper corner of the picture, alerting the projectionist. He would stand ready beside the off-duty machine until the flash of a second circle. Then he'd turn that machine on and the first one off, so swiftly and smoothly that most of the audience remained unaware of the change.

One reason I was always welcomed into the booth was that my watchful eye at the catbird seat freed the projectionist to do other things, to work at the film splicer on the workbench behind the seat, or talk on the phone, or read or nap in the office behind the booth.

Stuart was working the booth tonight. For the first few years I'd known him I'd been in love with him. By now the love had simmered down to a comfortable, warm crush, which both of us recognized and enjoyed without wanting to activate it.

Stuart was the first rich person I'd ever known, and that had been part of the fascination at first. His mother, a wealthy widow who lived in a town house on Grand Avenue, owned much of downtown West Des Moines, including the building that housed the little theater. Managing the theater had been Stuart's first assignment when he'd been little older than I was now, and he'd kept control of the theater for years, even though he was now managing the family fortune. Like me, Stuart simply loved the warm, family feeling of the little neighborhood theater, and he loved the movies themselves.

He was a trim, good-looking man in his late thirties, whose face never completely lost its smile and who bounced when he walked. His wife was from his own social level but was a plain-looking woman, kind and pleasant and unfailingly thoughtful. One of their little boys had died of a heart defect; the other had cerebral palsy. Stuart often brought him to the theater on Saturdays to watch the children's matinee from the catbird seat.

"Time," I called as the circle flashed in the corner of the screen.

Stuart came out of the office, where he'd been taking marquee letters from their storage bins. Saturday night was change-the-marquee night. He moved to the silent projection machine and stood with his hand on its switch while he peered at the screen through the trap door. The second circle flashed. He threw switches; the beam of picture light jumped sideways as the new machine took over. Then he began the complicated process of unthreading the used reel and replacing it with the next. He'd shown me how to run the machines once.

I followed him back to the cramped office and stretched out on the sofa, an ugly, red plastic thing with chrome arms. Stuart finished taking the huge metal letters from their bins, then sat in the desk chair, with his feet on the sofa near mine, his hands behind his head.

84

"Well," he said, "another four months and you'll be graduating. I suppose that means I'll be losing you." He sounded genuinely sorry.

"I guess. I still don't know for sure what I want to do. Isn't that awful? Everybody else knows what college they're going to or what kind of job they're going to get, or whatever. I still . . . I just don't know. Nothing seems to fit right."

We'd talked about this before. Now, as before, Stuart said, "Trust your instincts, girl. Don't get into anything that doesn't feel right to you."

I pulled my shoulders up around my ears. "The school principal keeps pushing me toward college. Keeps telling me not to waste my life. I don't know, Stuart. It's such a big decision. I don't want to make the wrong choice."

"Well, my dear," he pontificated, "the first thing you have to do is quit worrying about making mistakes. At seventeen, you've got plenty of time to make more than one false start and still end up making a good life for yourself. What about college? What is it that turns you away from that direction?"

I shrugged. "Nothing I can explain. I've just, well, hated high school. I've always been such a flop socially. You know what I mean. No dates, no friends I really like, and I hate the confinement. Sitting in a room, studying, all that stuff. I don't think I'm lazy, exactly . . ."

"Just not academic. There's nothing wrong with that. Listen, the world is full of people who didn't fit into the college mold but who went on to have very successful,

85

happy lives. Maybe marriage will be the answer for you."

"I don't think marriage should be that kind of an answer for anybody. I mean, I think you need to be a whole person going into marriage. You shouldn't expect the marriage to make you whole."

He looked at me with startled respect.

I went on. "I've been thinking about going out to Denver after graduation. Jeanette said I could stay with her and Bob till I get a job and can afford a place of my own."

He studied my face with fatherly concern for a moment and said, "One trick I learned: When I'm trying to make a decision, I'll pretend to decide it one way, then I'll pretend to decide it the other way. I almost always get a gut-level reaction after the decision is made, either a feeling that it's right or a feeling that it's wrong. Try it out. Decide to go to college, and see how that feels. Then decide to go to Denver, and see how that feels."

He watched my face while I tried it. College . . . Denver . . .

My face cleared and lightened. Suddenly I stood up and stretched, then bent over him and gave him a quick peck on the forehead. "Thanks, father figure. You're not half bad for a rich guy, you know it?"

"Watch it," he snapped. "You'll make an old man die of heart failure, doing things like that. If I were forty years younger I'd get up and chase you around the office."

I snorted. "If you were forty years younger you'd be

prenatal." From the office door I looked back at him lovingly.

I went back to the viewing window but didn't sit down. Suddenly I was restless. I was tired of waiting for life to get started; I wanted to make something happen.

The theater below was narrow, just one center aisle with seats eight deep on either side. Although it was Saturday night, the weather was bad and most of the seats were empty. Down front near the screen, Charlotte and Diane slouched, knees on the seat backs in front of them. Bruce Whiteside was there alone, sitting halfway back against the wall. Mary Valdez and her current boyfriend were in the darkest back-row corner, and on the other side Roberto sat with two of his younger brothers.

I should go down there, I thought. Charlotte and Diane knew I was up in the booth and would be expecting me to come and sit with them for the last show. But I didn't want to. I got neck aches and crossed eyes sitting that close to the screen, and I was too restless to be content with their company.

I could go down and sit with Bruce, I told myself. He's there all alone; maybe he'd like company. On the other hand, if he wants my company all he has to do is ask me to go to the show with him. No, he's probably alone because he wants to be.

I scanned the crowd again and spotted Hazel Stott, also sitting alone against the wall. I could go down and sit with her, I knew. She'd probably be grateful for my company. But maybe not. Maybe it would seem condescending. We'd worked together in ninth grade over our biology specimens. She'd even helped me with my ink drawing of the frog's muscle system, but she withdrew instantly from any small gesture of friendship I'd made, jokes or a bit of offered gossip. I took the hint and kept the partnership strictly business.

I could go down and sit with Roberto, I knew, and he'd have welcomed me easily and naturally. I'd done it before. But always when he came to the theater it was with one or more of his brothers and sisters, and they were inclined to poke each other and point to me and make loud whispered jokes about Roberto's girlfriend.

In the end I settled on the catbird seat.

/ • /

Senior banquet and prom night. One of life's magic moments. I sat in the front seat of the car and looked over at my date—Charlotte Yoder.

Struggling to do right by us all, the class officers, Alton and Patricia and their friends, had voted to combine the banquet and prom on the same evening, so that the ones without dates for the prom would come to the banquet anyway and maybe stay for the prom. Office bulletins had stressed that the prom was not necessarily a date affair. We were all graduating seniors; we all had an equal right to enjoy our prom.

But of course it didn't work that way in real life. The ones who were stuck without dates would go to the banquet, then disappear. And we could be readily identified by our clothes. Prom girls wore long, pastel dresses of net and chiffon, with little net scarves standing away from their shoulders and rosebud corsages on their daringly strapless bosoms. The rest of us wore banquet clothes, our Easter suits with linen pumps dyed to match. Garter belts dug into our rumps and left coin-shaped indentations in our thighs.

I rested my hands on the Dodge's steering wheel and looked across at Charlotte for a full minute before pulling away from her curb. This was my fate. Not Bruce Whiteside pinning a corsage on my shoulder and standing grinning in the living room while Mom took pictures of her daughter in prom formal, with date and flowers.

No, what I had was Charlotte Yoder, and the use of the Dodge.

She had come drifting back toward me during this last year. No one in Pep Club or Glee Club had proved an adequate oak for her, I figured. I'd been stung by her drifting away but had done very little to get her back, feeling that it was somehow inappropriate for Joanne Herne to pursue Charlotte Yoder. She could pursue me and hang annoyingly on to me, and that was acceptable. For me to lower myself to chase her was not.

By our senior year almost everyone in the graduating class was paired with someone else, everyone except me and Charlotte, and Diane, who was still diligently at work trying to break up Carolyn and Dale. Only the worst and dumbest of us were left single, and Hazel Stott, of course. All of the top-level girls were going steady, pinned, openly engaged or expecting rings on prom night.

Over and over through the months leading up to tonight I'd anguished over myself. The flaw was there, somewhere. It had to be. I couldn't see it, I couldn't ask anyone to point it out to me, but it had to be there. Other, less attractive girls had boyfriends by now. Almost all had at least managed to snag a prom date from a not-great boy who also dreaded exclusion.

But not I.

I had tried. I had studied Bruce's movements for days so that I'd know when he went back to his locker and which door he left by in the afternoons. I perfected my timing and managed to be on the side-door steps tying a lace on my saddle shoe as he came out alone after speech practice.

"Hi," I said, standing up awkwardly.

He slowed and shifted his eyes away from mine and managed, "Hi."

"These darn shoelaces. I think I'll go back to penny loafers."

"Yeah," he said, and began edging around me.

"Uh, Bruce?"

He hesitated.

My face grew hot. "You going to the prom?" God, how obvious could I be? I was gambling so much. He still had no girlfriend, and his eyes occasionally locked on mine in a classroom, but that was not enough of a base for this kind of daring.

"Nah, I don't think so," he said.

We stared at each other, unable to break the spell of utter discomfort. Then the door opened and a herd of boys came out, and he went off with them.

I played sick the next day so I wouldn't have to face him.

"Well," Charlotte said, "are we going to sit here all night, or are we going to our banquet?"

I rammed the Dodge into gear and we were off.

The banquet was my first experience with fine dining. It was held at the country club. The table was set with thick linens and heavy silver, and for a while I forgot the distinction between prom dresses and Easter suits. We all looked beautiful. Even Roberto in his shiny black suit and with his silly behavior seemed to have turned into an adult—just since history class yesterday.

As I settled into my place at the table I felt surprisingly at home. Charlotte was fussing with the napkin rings and salad forks, but I felt right, here with all the linen and silver and floral centerpieces. Did that mean I was a superior person? To the manor born? I'd have been tempted to think so, if not for the proof of my inferiority given to me every day by the boys who looked past me.

We were seated at round tables, one teacher for each table. This banquet was to introduce us gently into finer living and heavy silverware. Although no one had instructed us, I assumed that we were to make polite conversation like grownups and show how well we could function on this level.

Since there was an endless wait between salad and the arrival of full dinner plates from the kitchen, I took a stab at the conversation. Start with the one who needs it most, I decided, and caught Hazel Stott's eye across the carnations.

"So where are you going, to college?" I asked her.

She shook her head. "Business school," she said in a low voice.

I was surprised. I'd figured her for college-bound if anyone was. She'd done nothing but study ever since I'd known her; I assumed she loved it. Maybe her family couldn't afford college. It came as a mild surprise to realize that I knew nothing about her family, not even what part of town they lived in.

Mentally I shrugged and moved on to the next face. Mary Valdez was as opposite from Hazel as she could be, I thought, with her beautiful creamed-coffee skin and black, bright eyes and bouncing ponytail. Her face smiled automatically, not from social necessity but from personal effervescence.

Of course she was happy. Why shouldn't she be? Everyone loved her. She was the center of every group in school, it seemed to me. Head cheerleader, chosen girlfriend of the brightest and handsomest of the Mexican boys. No isolation in her life.

"How about you?" I asked her. "Where are you going?"

She paused for dramatic effect, then grinned widely. "Our Lady of the River."

A Catholic college? I'd never heard of it.

But Mrs. Mahoney, who was our table's teacher, pulled in her breath and stared at Mary. "You're going to be a nun? Oh, Mary . . ." her voice faded into embarrassed dismay.

A nun?

We all stared at the girl who had been our bright light all these years.

"Yep," she said with utter satisfaction. "That's where I figure I'll do the most good in the world, so that's where I'm going."

After a stunned pause, during which dinner plates finally began to arrive at our table, the question was passed on. Diane was going to Iowa State to work toward a teaching degree. Charlotte and I knew she'd chosen Iowa State because that was the school Carolyn had selected from among her basketball scholarship offers.

Doug Hempel was going to a trade school and then into his father's plumbing business. Marvin Gates would work full time at the Standard station. Donny Braumeister was going to UCLA.

"Joanne?" Mrs. Mahoney passed the question to me.

"I don't know yet what I want to do," I said. "I decided not to start college till I knew what career I wanted, so I'm going out to Denver after graduation, and stay with my sister for a while, get a job, try to decide."

Mrs. Mahoney nodded, as though she found that a fitting answer. A small flare of protest heated me. She shouldn't have lumped me with the noncollege ones. I was the second smartest in the class; didn't she remember?

No, of course not. It probably wasn't even true. What do IQ tests prove anyhow?

After the banquet, the school superintendent rose and gave a brief speech full of jokes he used year after year. Then, special awards. I turned my chair to a more comfortable position, knowing there would be no special awards for Joanne Herne, who had kept her light hidden under a bushel throughout her school years . . . if she had a light at all.

First, the formal announcement of valedictorian and salutatorian. The ultimate honor went to . . .

Hazel Stott.

I clapped along with everyone else while Hazel's eyes burned with a hard angry fire. Defiance? Revenge on us all? I stared at her.

The honor of being salutatorian went to . . .

Bruce Whiteside.

Again I clapped. I felt estranged and passed over; not envious, but acutely aware that I could have had one of those honors if I'd tried for it. Hazel had needed it more than I, and she had grimly passed both Bruce and me to get it.

Suddenly I looked over at her and smiled with the first genuine warmth I'd ever shown her. Good for you, Hazel Stott, I thought, and applauded her in my head. She knew what she wanted and she got it.

"Citizenship Award," continued the superintendent. "This award is given every year to the graduating student who has contributed the most unselfishly to our community. It makes me very proud to give this plaque to a student who has given hundreds of hours of volunteer time, over the past three years, to working with handicapped children at Mercy Hospital and at Camp Sunnyside. Good work, Roberto Rodriguez."

Roberto did a burlesque shuffle up to the speakers' table to accept the plaque. When he was handed the mike and told to say a few words, he drew himself up tall and said, "A few words. Thank you." And jigged back to his seat.

Roberto? Silly old Roberto, spending hundreds of unpaid hours lifting kids in and out of wheelchairs? Why? I stared at him, fascinated.

I had an overwhelming urge just then to get up and go to him and give him a giant hug, though I didn't know why. He just seemed to make up for so much that was bad or inadequate about the rest of us.

The banquet ended, the pastel formals went off in polished cars toward the Val Air ballroom, and Charlotte and I went home.

/ 7 /

As the plane coasted down toward the runway, I felt a familiar nervous tingle in my stomach. Over the past eight or ten years I'd become a fairly popular speaker at writers' workshops, and I'd outgrown the awful stage-fright of the early speeches. But I retained this tingle of nerves when I'd come into a new airport, where I would be met by a strange committee member and stared at covertly for a day or so: Jo Herne, author of all those books.

I smiled at myself as I unsnapped my seatbelt prematurely. Silly to be nervous about this trip. This was only going home again, seeing a lot of middle-aged people whom I used to know slightly in a previous existence. None of them was important to me now, no matter how important they might have been decades ago. And I was of no importance to them, nor had I ever been. I was the observer looking in the window; they had been the ball players and cheerleaders. They had been the tigers.

Standing with my head bent under the overhead storage compartment, waiting for the passengers already standing in the aisle to move forward, I wondered whether I would still be an outsider. If I was, it wouldn't hurt me now. I'd made a wonderful, enviable life for myself. I wouldn't be anyone but me, if I could choose. This self-built happiness gave me invulnerability against the kind of wounding the fifteen-year-old Jo had known.

Okay, tigers, here I come.

The line began to move, the flight attendant bade us each a nice day at the door, and I was out, moving through the terminal on a surge of pent-up energy. Sitting in planes always affected me that way.

I picked up my rental car from Hertz and drove to the motel near the airport, where I had reserved a room. The reunion banquet would be held in one of the motel's party rooms on Saturday night. I'd booked my room there so I could have a few drinks at the party if I felt inclined, without having to drive afterward. I drank so little and so seldom that a glass of wine was enough to affect my vision and reflexes, and I held a solid loathing for people who drove even a little bit drunk.

I checked into my room, kicked off my traveling shoes, and pondered. It was a little after five, Friday night. According to the flyer sent out by the reunion committee, Friday night was a kick-off party. Eight o'clock at the Legion Hall; come in fifties clothes. Sat-

97

urday was golf, volleyball, or free time to get together with special friends. Saturday night, the big dress-up banquet, and Sunday a picnic at Valley Park.

My own plans were: the party tonight, shopping tomorrow or swimming in the motel pool, probably alone, the banquet tomorrow night, then home on the early flight Sunday. Two evenings of rehashing old times that hadn't been that great in the first place were plenty.

I looked out my window at the motel pool and debated. It was hot out there, the old heavy, humid, August-in-Iowa heat I'd nearly forgotten after all these years high and dry in my Arizona valley. A swim would feel good, and I'd remembered to bring my suit, thanks to Theo's reminder.

On the other hand, there were half a dozen noisy, splashing children in the pool, I'd forgotten my hair dryer, and the fifties party was less than three hours away. I didn't want to make my grand entrance with damp, stringy hair. On a sigh, I turned on the television for company and had a shower instead of a swim.

My fifties costume consisted of the only thing I could put together without sewing something, which would have been too much trouble: jeans with rolled-up cuffs, knee sox rolled down into the bulky bobby-sox cuffs that had uglified the legs of my generation, loafers, a white man-style shirt with the tails untucked. There now. The old me.

I laughed at the woman in the mirror. My hair had been white since my early thirties, and I loved it that way, but its short-cropped silvery waves looked odd above the bobby-soxer clothes. My skin was deep brown and dried to a patina of fine leather, and there was a sag to the underjaw. Other than those minor flaws, that fifty-year-old in the mirror was no slouch. Looking head-on, the little bit of extra belly didn't show, and all the rest of it was firm and healthy.

What would Charlotte look like, I wondered. Chubby, for sure. She'd had that roundness about her limbs and features even in fifth grade. At fifty she could hardly have escaped it. Suddenly I was curious, eager to see all those faces in the yearbook. With a writer's instinct I tried to extend their lives in my imagination, to see where they had gone and how happily they had turned out. Patricia Winston? Was hers still a charmed life? Had Roberto found a job and a wife that suited him? Had Mary Valdez really become a nun?

"We shall see," I told the handsome Arizona woman in the mirror, and I left.

Supper was a solitary picnic at Waterworks Park. Not wanting to be seen in public in the bobby sox and rolled-up jeans, I'd swung through a Hardee's drive-up window and got a bag of cholesterol to take to the park. Chewing the last delicious onion ring, I drove east through downtown Des Moines, on our old scoop-the-loop route. How many nights had Charlotte, Carolyn, Diane, and I driven these streets after roller skating or after a school game, eyeing boys in passing cars, hoping for romance. Down Locust Street toward the glorious gold-domed capitol building shining across the river, then back west again on Walnut, all the way through downtown and home again past the mansions of Grand Avenue, disappointed but safe.

The chances we took, ignorant of the risks of rape and murder; I shook my head now, thinking of them.

The city had changed in the twenty years since my last visit. There were twinkle-lighted trees growing along the sidewalks now, handsome buildings and plazas and sculpture. My city, I thought, and surprised myself.

West along Grand Avenue, past the governor's mansion, past stately homes and new insurance buildings and finally, sixty blocks later, down the long hill into West Des Moines. Valley Junction it was in its early years, and Valley Junction it was again, now that it was a smart suburb with its pseudo-quaint shopping center.

The Friday-evening commuter traffic carried me faster than I wanted to go. I craned for a glimpse of the bowling alley, the Val Air ballroom where I hadn't gone to the prom. There was the gas station where Charlotte and I had pooled our quarters for a dollar's worth of gas to scoop the loop in Daddy's Dodge.

It was only seven, too early to go to the Legion Hall, where the party was to be. I drove west on Grand, up the hill that formed the far side of the Valley, past the Methodist church my parents' fund-raising committee had helped build. I detoured a block south to see the schools, but they were gone. Their block was empty except for sidewalks that outlined the razed buildings. Of course. The town had spread west now. That's where the new schools would be. The old buildings had probably become tax and insurance expenses.

I felt oddly empty. It was like going to a funeral for

someone lost at sea. If you couldn't see the body, you couldn't quite believe the life was over.

North on Eighth Street, I tried to follow my memories to the old riding stable. The gravel road I'd pedaled over, on all those steamy summer afternoons, was a broad and crowded thoroughfare now. Shopping centers lined it and a major four-lane highway soared over it. The houses that supplanted the woods near the stables didn't even look like new houses. Their trees were large, their driveways patched.

Circling on a baffling grid of wide, busy roads, I found my way back to the old, familiar part of West Des Moines and swung over to Eleventh Street. The house of my high school years was painted a different color. Its trees, too, were large. The house seemed smaller and shabbier than I remembered.

Down the hill, past the elementary school, which still looked exactly as I remembered it except that the play area was paved now. A shame to pave a play area. Grass is a child's natural habitat. Past Charlotte's old house, which looked truly shabby now. Past our old house on Sixth and Elm. I pulled over and looked at it for a while. This part of town was still as quiet as it had been forty years ago. I liked it much better than the new subdivisions. The house had shrunk, as I suppose all childhood places do, but otherwise looked much as it had on the day when we'd led the moving van down from Kendallville.

Across the street was the old Schultz's Grocery, where Mom had collared Charlotte for me. It was an antique refinishing shop now.

Eight o'clock. Time to go into the tiger's den. Time

to play rich and famous author returning to her school-mates, the unexpected success of the class of '55.

The nervous tingle was back in my belly.

/ • /

The American Legion Hall was in the major block of Main Street, just down from my father's old office. Going through the glass-brick entry, I had dim memories of community Halloween parties here. My dentist's office had been down the corridor and to the left.

I turned right, into a long, narrow, brightly lit room where twenty or thirty people milled. The floor was linoleum, the walls painted some dull institutional color, the furniture a pair of long Masonite tables and a rim of gray metal folding chairs around the walls. Shades of junior-high dances. I grinned.

Balloons and streamers brightened the ceilings, though, and on the walls were long computer printouts that said, "GO TIGERS, IF YOU STILL CAN," and "HAPPY FIFTIETH BIRTHDAY TO US ALL."

At the table beside the door sat a woman whose face was distantly familiar. Patty? Patsy? Something like that. She'd been one of the fat girls no one had noticed back then. She was still plump, but maturity validated a shape that had instilled shame in a sixteen-year-old. Now she looked smiling, confident, very much in charge of her sign-in book and her array of name tags.

She knew me immediately and greeted me like an old friend. "I hear you're writing books now. That's just great. Glad somebody in the old gang turned out famous."

102

Her voice was genuinely warm, with no hint of envy in it. As I peeled the paper backing from my name tag and slapped it onto my shirt, I decided that her life must have turned out okay. Miserable people don't greet rich and famous classmates with that calm, clear-faced smile. Good for her, I thought.

"Joanne, yay!" The voice had not changed in thirty years. I turned and collided with Charlotte's hug. We held each other off by the shoulders and looked.

Obviously I wasn't going to be the only well-preserved fifty-year-old in the group. Charlotte had plumped out just enough to keep the smooth youthful sheen on her skin. Her glasses had been replaced by contact lenses, her pale hair was a long mass of kinks more befitting a college girl than a middle-aged woman. She seemed revved up with excitement. I'd never seen her so animated.

She pulled me toward a snack-and-drink bar in the corner, but the going was slow. Teasingly familiar faces turned to me as I made my way through the standers and talkers. We searched each other's faces, stole peeks at name tags, then laughed and said, "I remember you. Donny Braumeister." "Joanne Herne! Hey, I hear you had some books published or something like that."

"Something like that." I grinned and moved on. Hey, this was fun. A strange feeling of homecoming washed over me, strange because I'd never felt at home with these people when we were children together.

Charlotte got a beer and bowl of popcorn, I fished a can of diet Coke from the tub of ice behind the snack bar, and we settled at one of the long, brown tables. I tried to remember Charlotte's last Christmas card. We'd dwindled off to Christmas cards within five years of graduation. I knew she'd stayed on at home, taken a job in the printing plant at Meredith Publishing, which had then been one of Des Moines's big employers of high school graduates in the fifties. I knew she'd married someone named Ray Berry and that they had moved to North Carolina.

"So," I said as we settled. "What have you been doing for the last twenty-five years?" A bubble of silliness was beginning to rise in me. "Just hit the highlights, now. I don't want to hear about all your sordid divorces and affairs."

She laughed. "No, I'm still married to Ray. Got three kids. I'm a grandmother, if you can believe it. Here, I just happen to have . . ." and out came the snapshots. "This is Tina, this one is the newest grandson, Matthew. Smart as a whip."

I shuffled through the pictures, made the right noises, couldn't stop grinning.

"We're still in Charlotte," Charlotte said. "Ray says we moved there so he'd remember my name. He's a real stitch. I wish you could meet him."

"He didn't come?"

"Nah, couldn't get off work."

"What does he do, again? I forgot."

"Works for IBM, servicing office machines. And I went back to work after the kids left home. I'm secretary to a real nice guy in an insurance office. Here's a picture of our house, and here's our boat that we got

104

last summer. It's not very big, but we go fishing a lot. We really enjoy it."

Fragments of her life floated past me. I tried to line them up and attach them to the girl I remembered, but there was too big a gap in the middle. With growing impatience I waited for her to ask me about my life. I wanted to let her know that I'd achieved the best possible existence for myself. But we were constantly interrupted by laughing faces peering at us and saying, "Hey, I remember you."

Restlessly, I got up while Charlotte showed her pictures to the woman across the table. I wanted to move around, make contact with everyone in the room.

An arm slipped around my waist. I turned and studied the balding head and sagging face at my shoulder. "Alton Grant?"

"The one and the same." He grinned and belched a gust of beer at me. "Hey, somebody told me you live out in Texas and write dirty books or something. Didn't you ever get married? Or are you between husbands?"

He nodded down at my maiden name pasted to my shirt.

I leaned a little away from his breath and looked him in the eye. "Never got married, Alton. Never found anybody good enough for me."

He bellowed, and everyone looked at him. From behind him came a dark-haired woman whose face was set in tension lines. Alton drew her up beside him and said, "Joanne Herne, like you to meet my wife,

Beverley Grant. Old Bev doesn't know it, but I used to have the hots for you in high school."

I snorted and shot his wife a look of apology and sympathy. As I unwrapped his arm from my waist I said, "Alton, I think you have me confused with three other girls. Excuse me."

I turned and started toward the rest room, more in need of a destination than relief. The silly grin still played across my face, and I didn't want Alton to think I was laughing at him. I was, of course. Pity his poor wife, I thought, and I shook my head at the agony I'd wasted, all those years ago, thinking I wasn't good enough for the Alton Grants of the world.

I collided with a tall, stout, masculine body. Bouncing off, I looked up into a round, brown face, and suddenly my grin took on new depth. On an impulse I reached up and hugged him, and he laughed and hugged me back.

"Good old Roberto."

"Good old Joanne."

I glanced around to see if there was a wife on his tail, and saw no one. Then I reared back for a better look. The years had made amazingly few changes in him. He seemed taller now, and his roundness was solidified into ordinary middle-aged stoutness. His skin was as smooth as a boy's, and his black eyes held the sparkle of the ten-year-old buffoon in 5-B. His name tag said "Dr. Roberto Rodriguez."

"Doctor?" I stared at the name tag with unflattering amazement. He threw back his head and laughed.

106

"Yeah, I kind of surprised everybody with that. Myself included."

"What kind of doctor?" I asked, remembering the dumb answers he used to give in class to make us laugh.

"Ph.D. kind. Not a brain surgeon or anything like that."

"But still," I glowed at him, "Roberto, a Ph.D., that is terrific. You know, I always suspected there were some smarts behind all that silliness you used to pull. What's your field? What do you do?"

"I'm a professor at Northwestern. I teach teachers of handicapped and special-ed children and do minority counseling."

We pulled up a pair of metal chairs and sat grinning foolishly at one another. I shook my head finally and said, "You old fox, how come you always acted like such a dummy in school?"

He shrugged and glanced away, and I could see a shade of the adolescent flit across his face. "When you're a fat boy of a minority race, you have to be a clown or something. Make them laugh with me so they don't laugh at me, you know, that sort of thing."

I lay my head to one side and said, "You know, I'm not really surprised. Now that I think about it, you always did have a kind of . . . I don't know . . . sensitivity toward other people's needs. A kind of tact. Empathy, I guess. I always had the feeling I could have told you anything terrible about myself and you would have understood. You were a humanitarian even in fifth

107

grade." I nodded firmly. "Yes, I think you ended up just right."

We laughed again. He asked about my life and I told him the outlines of it.

"You turned out just right, too," he said warmly. "I always knew you were a special person. You just had that air about you. Like you knew where you were going in life and didn't need anybody's help."

I'd just started a sip of Coke and sputtered it all over him. "My God, Roberto. You didn't really think that, did you?"

"Oh, sure. Everybody did."

I stared. "Well, I certainly had you all fooled then. I had no idea who or what I was back then, and I was scared of everybody. I felt totally out of it, all through school."

"No," he said, unbelieving. "So did I."

"No." I echoed him, and we were off again on a roll of laughter.

We separated then, to continue our games of "Hey, I remember you." And a game it was, each of us peering into faces, trying to find names for them in our memories. I looked for Mary Valdez, wondering if she had gone through with her plan to become a nun. She wasn't there.

Standing against the wall an hour or so later, I scanned the room and made a mildly surprising observation. Of the forty to fifty of us in the room, only Alton Grant was of the ruling class. The others the worker bees, the mid and lower levels of the social strata, as we had sorted ourselves or been sorted back then. Interesting, I thought. It should have been the in crowd, with their golden-glowing memories of high school days, who would want to come back to reminisce. Instead, here were the out-of-its, rising now to run the show and to laugh together about remember-the-time. Odd.

I said as much to Roberto when he drifted up beside me.

"Not so surprising," he chuckled. "Those were the kids who everybody thought would have charmed lives. You know, it all came so easily to them when they were young. The pretty girls, the sons of lawyers. I just have a hunch that when they got out into the real world, they weren't as well equipped to handle it as the rest of us were. Girls like that, Patricia Winston and those others, grow up thinking that all they have to be is pretty, that they don't need to put themselves out any more than just what it takes to catch a husband with good prospects, and then they can coast the rest of the way through life. Those are the ones who end up going through marriages left and right, drinking too much, aging too fast. You know the old saying: early ripe, early rotten. If their lives didn't turn out to their own glorified expectations and everyone else's, I can see why they wouldn't be so eager to come back and be seen."

I thought about it. "You could be right."

"On the other hand," he motioned around the room, "you take these women here, Patsy Beebe and some of those others. They weren't attractive back then, they suffered a lot, but then later their lives got better. Patsy's husband—that's that guy behind her in the cowboy

109

boots—is a great guy. A little weird, a little funny look-ing, but heck, they've been married all this time, still appreciate each other, still have a good time together. She didn't start out with anything like the expectations of the pretty girls, and when a little happiness came her way, she grabbed it, she appreciated it, and she took care of it. If you follow me."

I nodded thoughtfully. "Roberto, what ever hap-pened to Mary Valdez, do you know? I always liked her so much."

"Sister Mary." His smile remained, but saddened. "She died four, five years back. She was at our first re-union, nine years ago. Just as crazy as ever, dancing around and singing and whooping it up. The religious life didn't knock the old spirit out of her, not one bit."

"I'm glad," I said fervently.

"She died someplace in Argentina, I think it was, or Nicaragua; I can't remember. She was in a nursing order down there, and I guess she got shot in some kind of terrorist uprising."

"Aw, no. Not Mary."

I remembered her leading the singing in the bus on our ninth-grade skip-day trip, sitting on Mrs. Ma-honey's knee, ponytail bouncing. "Beer, beer for old Valley High," we sang, knowing nothing. I remembered her on the return trip, voicing compassion for Patricia's humiliation when the rest of us were snickering smugly. My eyes misted a little at the world's loss of that fine person, and Roberto looked away as if to hide his own misting eyes.

Late in the evening I noticed a tidy-looking couple

near the door, pasting name tags onto each other. Her face rang no bells in my memory, but something about his . . . I moved over to them and boldly read his name tag.

Bruce Whiteside. And, of course, his wife.

Although I'd drunk nothing but Cokes all evening, I was feeling not only silly but brash. "Bruce Whiteside," I said. "My first big love. Were you aware that I had a crush on you for approximately eight of my formative years?" I winked at his wife, who returned my smile good-naturedly.

He recognized me without having to read my chest. "Joanne Herne. Did you realize I had a crush on you? I just hadn't gotten to the point where I could talk to girls yet, and you scared the pants off me, you were so self-controlled."

"I was what?" My jaw dropped.

He took his wife's hand and said, "This is my wife, Loretta. Joanne Herne."

I looked at them both. They matched. He was much taller than he'd been as a boy, and he was strikingly good looking in a quiet way. His hair was full and dark and probably genuine, and the extra padding of mature flesh brought his narrow face into balance. His features were neat, unlined, contented; his smile was genuine.

Loretta, too, was slim and dark haired and groomed. She had the look of an intelligent woman living a life that suited her.

I moved with them toward the bar, and as we went, we exchanged facts of lives. Bruce was an administrator at a small private college in Ohio. Loretta was dean of women there. Their one child was doing graduate studies in London.

As they talked I began to picture their lives. Their house would be full of books and artifacts from their summer travels. Their friends would be other faculty families, their world bounded by the college. Just right for them; a disaster for me.

If I had prevailed in my fight for his attention, we might have gone off to college in tandem. I might have married him and become a faculty wife. Probably I never would have found the time, the energy, the need, to write that first book. I would have evolved into Loretta instead of Jo Herne, the Arizona writer. But it would not have fit, that life of Loretta Whiteside's. It would never have fit me. I'd have rebelled against the petty strictures of academic life. I'd have gone on dreaming my dream of riding over the mountain, instead of living it. My face now would be drawn with tension, like Alton Grant's wife's.

How lucky it was for all of us that Bruce's instincts had shielded him from me.

By the end of the evening I'd spent several more short periods with Charlotte at the table, I'd danced with Roberto and Bruce and Alton and men I barely remembered, and I'd come to the happy conclusion that all of us had somehow turned out just as we were meant to.

The comfortable, at-home mood stayed with me, puzzling but nice. These people were like sisters or cousins; they had known me from the beginning of my life and they were a part of the fabric of it, just as Theo and

Ginny were. They were, perhaps, the warp of the weaving, across which the later patterns were worked, without which those later patterns would have unravelled.

For I could see clearly that all of us now, in middle age, were the inevitable results of our beginnings. Our individual natures were no doubt shaped by the events and relationships of our youths, but those natures prevailed in the end.

We did not change as we grew older; we just became more clearly ourselves.

/ 8 /

"What about that Alton Grant? Aren't we glad we didn't get hooked up with him?" Charlotte laughed.

It was Saturday afternoon. We'd been swimming in the motel pool, me doing my fairly graceful dives in the deep end and Charlotte paddling in the shallow water, straining to keep her hair dry. My own white thatch was drying under mother nature's giant dryer in the sky. We lay sprawled on lounges made of narrow cords of brown and white plastic. I had arranged the belt of my robe across my eyebrows as a sun shield; Charlotte stayed in the shade of a tree.

"All in all," I said judiciously, "I'd say our whole group aged very well. I still can't believe we are actually fifty years old. I mean, *I'm* not fifty years old except maybe for my body."

"I know it. Remember when we used to wonder what

it would be like to be old, thirty, forty? We couldn't even imagine fifty."

Some of the old camaraderie was coming back now in my feelings toward Charlotte. We were independent of each other, each secure in her own life, free to explore thoughts together as we'd never been in the early years.

I mused aloud. "You know, kids are funny. There we were, all those years, best friends, and I don't recall that we ever actually talked. Do you? I mean, our friendship was so superficial. I have women friends in my life now who are so much closer to me than you and I ever got, and I'm sure you do, too. I wonder why we wasted all that potential?"

She opened one eye and said, "I never thought of it that way. I thought we were very close back then. I don't think I've ever had a closer friend than you were."

Silently I thought, Poor Charlotte, if that's all she's ever been capable of. Oh well, of course our friendships were superficial back then. We weren't old enough for anything else. We hadn't been through the kinds of experiences that create the deeper friendships.

I thought about Theo and Ginny, about Ginny's death.

Our thoughts wandered. After a while Charlotte said, "Didn't you ever get married, Jo? Even briefly? Or come close?"

I chuckled. "I was engaged a few times. When I was living in Denver that year after high school, I got engaged to an air force guy, someone Jeanette's husband knew. We only went out a few times, and I suppose he was lonesome or scared of life or something, so he proposed, and I said yes because I figured I might never get asked again. You know how wise we were at eighteen. But then he started telling me how things were back where he came from, which was west Texas someplace. The menfolk ate at the table and the womenfolk served and ate in the kitchen. He didn't believe in store-bought bread, and breakfast had to be a meat-and-potatoes meal."

"What a turkey. Was that your only close call?" Her voice was soft and distant, as though she wanted my conversation only as a lullaby.

"Oh, no. There were a few others over the years, but I tell you, the older I got, the more accustomed I got to the luxury of living alone, and finally one day I woke up to the fact that I was just plain not intended to go through life in double harness. It wasn't right for me. From that point on, I just relaxed and started living my life the way I genuinely wanted to, instead of keeping everything on hold, waiting for Mister Right."

"How did you get started writing, anyway?" Still her voice was faraway, unconcerned.

"I was driving around the mountains west of Boulder one weekend. I was still living in Denver, if you remember. Jeanette and Bob had been transferred to Okinawa, but I stayed on in Denver, working at the phone company. I was up to supervisor by then and I was making decent money, but I hated cities and apartments, and I was getting so . . . frustrated. I felt as if my life was passing me by and I hadn't yet found the big wonderful thing I wanted to be doing with it. I was around twenty-four then."

"That was about when we quit sending Christmas cards."

"Right. Anyhow, I went up to Boulder that weekend, just cruising the mountain roads, daydreaming about living there, and I saw this sign: 'Rocky Mountain Western Writers Conference.' So just on an impulse I drove up there and crashed it. It was some kind of private lodge, I think, and here were these little discussion groups scattered around under the pine trees. Nobody knew who I was, so I spent the whole afternoon sitting in on these discussion groups. They were talking about things like the best methods of research and how to find a good agent and techniques for creating tension by paragraphing. Oh, and how to work it so you get tax deductions for working at home. The whole thing just fascinated the hell out of me.

"The idea of being a writer had crossed my mind from time to time before that, I suppose. I was always happiest when I was reading. But the thing that stopped me from even considering it seriously was my . . . self-image. I couldn't imagine ordinary, no-college Jo Herne doing anything as awesome as writing a book. Yet I sat there that afternoon, with all of these incredibly ordinary people around me and they were writing books, or trying to. I could tell from the discussions that they weren't any smarter than I was. Some of them were downright strange." I chuckled.

"But the thing was," I went on more seriously, "as I sat at that writer's conference I had the feeling, for the very first time in my whole life, that I actually fit in with the people around me. It was an incredible experience. This group was people who wrote books or stories set in the West, and that got me to remembering all those western books I used to love, Zane Grey and all

117

those. And I just suddenly knew. There was no doubt in my mind. I was going to write a western novel, somebody was going to publish it, and after a few years I'd be able to support myself just by writing. I'd move someplace in the mountains and live exactly the life I'd always fantasized in the back of my mind.

"So I did it. It took about seven years of working days and writing evenings before I had enough books out to make a living from it, but that was one of the happiest times of my life. I quit my job as soon as I could and moved near Aspen for a while. I stayed in different people's ski lodges and took care of them for the owners, kept vandals out, stuff like that. And then I had this writer friend in Phoenix, and I moved down there and lived with her for a while till we got on each other's nerves. By that time my books were earning pretty well, so I bought the place I've got now, and I'll never leave there till they carry me out feet first."

I waited for her to compliment me on my achievements.

She was asleep.

When she woke, I decided not to bother trying to talk to her about my life. Instead I said, "Okay now, Charlotte, tell me the real stuff. You can't have just gotten married and lived happily ever after. I mean, you must have had some rough patches."

Knowing now the strength and beauty of women's friendships, I suppose I was testing her depths, curious to know what might have been possible for us.

"Oh, we didn't have much money in those early years," she said. "When we first got married I was still working at Meredith, of course, and Ray was working at the post office. We had that horrible little trailer out on Army Post Road. I think you were over there one time, at Christmas, weren't you?"

I shook my head.

"Well, anyway, then I got sick of that boring, stupid job, and I got pregnant so I wouldn't have to work. Then Ray got on with IBM as a trainee and went off to training school for six months. He wasn't even home when Tina was born. He still wasn't earning enough, so he got a night job at the *Des Moines Register* in the printing room. He kept wanting me to go back to work, but heck, I'd got started watching soap operas by that time. I couldn't go back to work." She laughed.

"Let's see, then I had Jason, then we bought that little house on Glover, then I had Kevin . . ."

The litany went on. I watched her with a detached kind of fascination.

". . . move to North Carolina, it was a big step up for Ray, and after that we didn't have the money worries . . ."

The way she stressed "money" made me suspect there had been other forms of worry.

She went on. "But then he started bowling with a league on Wednesday nights. At least, that was what he said he was doing. Actually he was having affairs; not just affair, singular, it was affairs, plural. It went on for years, different women, mostly secretaries who worked in the offices where he was doing his repair jobs. He'd been having these Wednesday-night flings for—get

119

this—six years before I accidentally found out he wasn't in a bowling league."

I couldn't help smiling. It wasn't nice of me to smile, but I couldn't help it. The shade from her tree was coming over onto my face now. I brushed the robe sash from my eyebrows and let my skin relax in its freedom from the sun's glare.

"So what did you do?" I asked. "Obviously you're still married."

"The only thing I could do, once he knew I was on to him. I gave him permission."

I opened one eye and cocked her a look. "You gave him permission?"

She nodded placidly. "I told him if he'd promise not to divorce me, he could go on having his Wednesday nights at the Holiday Inn as long as he wanted to, no questions asked."

"And it worked?" I asked, mildly incredulous.

"Of course it worked. In fact, he only went out a couple more times after that, and then he quit doing it. Maybe it wasn't so exciting when he didn't have to sneak and lie anymore. I don't know. Maybe he was just getting tired of it. Or getting old, so it wasn't as easy to get the pretty young girls anymore."

"And then you lived happily ever after?" I asked cheerfully.

"Yep."

"Well, good for you."

We closed each other out again with our eyelids, and I thought about varying kinds of strength. I thought about ivy outlasting the oak trees it grows on.

/ 9 /

My silliness bubble started to swell again as I walked into the Walnut Room down the hall from the motel's lobby. It was the senior banquet at the country club all over again, only this time the senior students were finished products with thinning hair and thickening waists, with disappointing jobs and marriages, and grandchildren in their wallets. Again I was an outsider looking in at them, but now I knew it was by choice. And I understood that it had been by choice back then, too. I was different. We all were. That didn't mean we weren't also kin.

With last night's party behind me, I found that I was beginning to absorb these people as they were now, rather than seeing them through an overlay of their childhood faces. Now the fun could begin, I thought, and danced a little shuffle step up to the inevitable table

121

with the inevitable name tags. Tonight the name tags were accompanied by tiny pin-on pink rosebuds. Should have been orange and black rosebuds. Yay, Tigers.

I was wearing my knock-'em-dead dress, red silky stuff with huge charcoal roses splashed all over it. It had a sort of oriental top, but ended in a flapper-style kicky swing at the knees. Usually I wore it on banquet nights at Western Writers' conferences, and every time I wore it I had a terrific time. Whether the dress was the cause or not I didn't know or care. I loved this dress, and I refused to sully it with a name tag or a teeny pink rosebud. The nametag I stuck on my forehead, the rosebud above my ear.

A man I remembered faintly swept me over to the bar with him and bought me a white wine, and we clotted with three or four others.

I said, "Can anyone tell me why it is that this strange class is having a reunion on their thirty-second year? And why we had our first one at twenty-three years? Why not fives, tens, and twenties like normal classes?"

The question was laughed around the room, becoming louder and louder, until the subject became general. Patsy of the name tag concession called back to me over the noise, "We started out to have a twenty-fifth year reunion, and the committee started in two years ahead of time, researching addresses. Only it didn't take as long as we thought, and then we decided, heck, if we wait two years half of these people will have moved, so we might as well hurry up and have the reunion while we know where you all are."

Laughter.

Roberto yelled back, "Then how come this one, nine years later?"

Patsy bellowed, "We had so much fun at the first one, we just rested up nine years and said hey, time for another one."

Someone else called, "I think we should stick to this schedule. I like the way people look at you funny when you tell them you're going to your thirty-two-year reunion. Heck, why be ordinary?"

"Yeah, anyone can have five-year reunions. Let's be different."

I called, "If we stick to this schedule, we'll have one at forty-one years, then one at fifty. Then let's quit while we're even with the world."

"Yeah, quit while some of us are still alive."

I glowed with a camaraderie I had never expected to feel with these people.

As the crowd thickened the air grew warmer, and my sweat loosened the name tag from my forehead. Ah well, what's in a name tag? If they didn't know me by then, who cared? I started to wad it up for a shot at a trash container, but then I stopped and ironed it and slipped it into my purse for a souvenir. I never did things like that.

Charlotte came in then, wearing something long and floral and looking almost pretty. Last night was for having fun together, but I knew that tonight was for showing ourselves off at our best. See how little I've aged? See how I've kept my figure, my hairline? See how happy and successful I am?

And of course I was doing it, too. Why not? Our

lives were our ultimate achievements. What could be more natural than to want to exhibit them, like crafts at a county fair, alongside the lives of the people we'd begun with? What fairer starting line in the race toward middle-age achievement than a small high school in a small town? We'd all been launched from the same education and at least reasonably equal family incomes. Our destinations were truly our individual trophies.

I followed Charlotte to one of the round dinner tables, feeling rather motherly and protective of her for no understandable reason. We were best friends all through school, however, and it was my responsibility to be sure she wasn't friendless here tonight.

At the table was a surprise. Carolyn. With a husband who wasn't Dale. We screeched politely and hugged, and dug in for abbreviated life stories. She and Dale had married in college, which I knew, and had taken coaching jobs in Seattle. Dale was caught in a scandal involving a girl student in the school where he taught, and they were divorced. He later married the girl and lived to regret it, Carolyn said with clear triumph. She introduced Greg, the second husband, who seemed pleasant enough, even though he was obviously bored. He looked exactly like Dale to me, but I kept my mouth shut.

"How are your family, your folks?" Carolyn asked me.

"Alive and well and living in Fort Lauderdale," I said. "They've got a little house down there, with a lanai and a canal going past the backyard, and bingo tournaments at their church. Mom's happy as a clam, but Daddy gets restless. You know him, he never learned how to do anything but work. He doesn't like to read or watch television, and there's never enough stuff around the house for him to fix. He just about drove Mom nuts when they first retired. He'd follow her all over the house criticizing things she'd been doing for fifty years. He didn't like her method of dusting furniture."

We all laughed and exchanged stories of retired parents. Carolyn said, "What ever happened to Jeanette and Judy?"

I liked her for asking. Charlotte hadn't bothered.

"Jeanette and Bob moved to Hawaii when he retired from the air force. They love it there. They're running a little gift shop on Maui. Judy is in Minneapolis, working as a set designer at the Guthrie Theater and loving it. She's between husbands at the moment, but that never lasts long with her."

The room was filling fast now. There were several old grads sifting into the crowd who had not been at last night's party. I shifted my chair and looked from face to face, trying to sort the classmates from the nontiger spouses.

One face snagged my attention, pulled me back for a harder look.

She came into the room alone, a slim, elegant figure in a black silk suit dramatically cut and draped. Rich brown hair was styled in full waves back from her face. The face. I stared, fascinated. It was small and small-featured but striking. Square, clean jawbone, smiling mouth, slim but dramatically curved eyebrows, placid gaze.

125

Hazel Stott.

"That's Hazel Stott," Charlotte whispered, astounded.

Carolyn replied, "That can't be Hazel Stott. That must be somebody's wife."

She was drifting through the room alone but with none of the discomfort most people show when coming alone into a full room. She carried herself like a queen. I grinned, untangled my feet from my purse straps, and got up.

"Hazel," I said, my voice bubbling with delight. "You look terrific. You must be having a wonderful life."

Her eyes met mine, and her smile warmed into something genuine and personal. "Joanne Herne. I hear you've become a successful author. I'm so proud of you. I always knew you were going to be the big achiever in our class."

I was so fascinated by her that I barely heard what she was saying. I found myself taking her hand, holding it, shaking it between us in some sort of victory gesture.

"Yeah, yeah, big deal. But Hazel, you look terrific!" I was aware that my words probably carried an element of insult, surprise at how the ugly duckling had swanified, but I couldn't help myself. I was delighted down to my toenails and I couldn't help spilling it out.

She cocked her elegant head just a shade to the side and said, "Yes, well, I'd had it with being the ugliest girl in the world. So I did something about it."

Dinner was announced then, and we were separated in the general flow of traffic along both sides of the buffet table.

126

I sat between Charlotte and Carolyn to eat, because my purse and my responsibility were at that table, but my mind stayed with Hazel. Good for her, I kept thinking. Good for her.

After dinner there were silly speeches by Alton Grant, as class president, and by Roberto, who had somehow become master of ceremonies. After an opening volley of jokes, though, Roberto showed us his serious professional self and made a moving tribute to Sister Mary Valdez. As he talked I could see both sides of the man, the chubby little boy who clowned for acceptance, and the portly professor who clowned sometimes to make a serious point. Intuitively I knew that the two sides of him were intermingled, that even now, within the safety of his professional and personal success, he was himself. One person, indivisible, with jokes and compassion for all.

I could love that man, I thought, misting over with the emotions of the evening. No, not really love him to the point of changing my life to conform to his; but, well, yes, love him in the broader sense. Love the kind of person he was. Love him as I loved Theo and Ginny and the precious scattering of special people who had spiced my life.

How odd, I thought, and smiled some more.

/ • /

It was after midnight. I unlocked my door down the hall from the banquet room and said, "Come on in."

I flipped on the light, kicked off the cruel shoes, and settled on the bed.

127

Hazel's shoes joined mine somewhere under the television, and she sank into the leatherette club chair beside the round table. We both carried our last party drinks, and I'd made off with half a bowl of popcorn from the banquet-room bar.

"Ah," I said, moving my toes in the luxury of release, "this is always the best part of the party. Now we can get down to serious talking."

After the speeches there had been dancing. Someone had made cassette tapes of old fifties records, and we two-stepped and jitterbugged our brains out. The flare at the bottom of my skirt was airborne for three solid hours. I'd loved it. I danced with Roberto and with two of the black men that unspoken rules had denied me access to when we were young. I danced with Charlotte in a parody of the old girls-with-girls dancing we'd done through high school, when the boys wouldn't ask us and we longed to join in. I danced three dances with Bruce Whiteside while his wife grinned confidently after us and Bruce told me about their son's graduate work in London. Such a handsome guy he'd turned out to be. Such a bore.

I danced with Alton Grant, who again confessed his early secret passion for me.

"Damn it, Alton," I'd yelled above the music, "where were you guys when I needed you? I went through all those years thinking I was a nothing because you stupid boys acted like I was. Don't come begging now, buddy. You're forty years too late, and I don't need you now."

He took it good-naturedly, thinking I was joking.

128

During the evening Charlotte and Carolyn had solidified in their marital mutuality, and I had moved to another table to sit with Hazel.

Now, in the silence of my room, we looked each other over once again and smiled.

"Okay," I said. "How did you do it? Where did you go after high school?"

"New York," she said flatly.

"You didn't go to college, then?"

She shook her elegant head. "I knew all through school that I was the ugliest one in the class, and I couldn't stand one more minute of it. I figured college would be four more years of the same and I couldn't face that. So I went to New York, signed up for a complete course at a charm school—what they called charm schools back then. It was like a modeling school, but lots of us weren't in it for modeling careers, we were just trying to . . . catch up, you know? I went into that place scared they were going to throw me out as hopeless, but you know what they told me? They told me I wasn't ugly. It was incredible. No one had ever before said that to me. They said I was not the ugliest person in the world, and I could be whatever I wanted to make myself into. Oh, yeah, sure, people are always telling kids that; but all of a sudden, I really understood it. Understood that it was true."

"So?" I urged, fascinated.

"So they showed me how to style my hair to balance the lines in my face and they changed my browline and taught me a whole bunch of little makeup tricks, and I got my teeth capped and straightened. My folks never wanted to spend the money on braces. I guess they thought it wouldn't do any good, the rest of me was so hopeless.

"The school taught me posture and carriage and how to sit and stand and walk gracefully. They taught me how to dress and how to smile so my gums didn't show, and how to hold eye contact when I talked to people. It was . . . magical, Jo. I began to look like royalty, just because of little things like head carriage and holding my hands and feet gracefully, and people treated me differently, as if I were a beautiful woman. It took a long time before I began truly feeling that way, but I made myself hold to the outward appearance, and gradually the inner change took place."

I just looked at her, smiling softly now. What courage this woman had. She was like Theo, I thought suddenly. They were women who suffered in hidden ways, women whose small, everyday acts of courage far exceeded my success as a writer.

"And then you got married," I prompted her. We'd exchanged bare facts between dances.

She nodded. "I went to work for the charm school for a few years, as a bookkeeper and then later as an instructor. Met John on a subway, got married three months later, and we're still on the honeymoon."

"Tell me about him."

She fished in her purse and brought up a picture. He was a small man, not good looking by any stretch of the imagination, but well-dressed and somehow gentle-seeming.

"He's a pediatrician. We live on Long Island now,

but we're seriously considering a move to Arizona or Nevada. He has emphysema, and the climate and pollution are really getting to him."

"He looks kind," I said, handing back the picture.

"Yes. He is. He's the kindest person I know, and the funny thing is, he'd have loved me just as much if I'd stayed homely. He was a homely kid growing up, too, so we know how to be gentle with each other's feelings. He gets a kick out of my looking terrific now, but he also understands. . . ."

"You were lucky," I said. "I counted an awful lot of second and third spouses around that room tonight. Not very many of them seem to have lucked out in that department."

We were thoughtful for a while.

Hazel said, "Tortoises and hares. The early leaders don't always go the course."

"I'd sure like to know how Patricia Winston turned out," I mused. "She was always the one who intimidated the socks off of me."

"Patricia Winston? Oh, she didn't bother me as much as some of the others did. She was just so far beyond me. On princess level. I figure if there's any justice she's probably a blowsy alcoholic by now."

I chuckled. "She's probably having a marvelous life in the Bahamas with diamonds from knuckle to knuckle and a millionaire husband, and just couldn't be bothered with piddling little class reunions."

We thought together in companionable silence.

"You know whom, of all the girls in our class, I was the most jealous of?" Hazel said finally. "You."

131

My jaw dropped. "Come on. Get real."

"No, I mean it. For me, Joanne Herne was the one who had it all. You were so poised all the time. Kind of quiet and self-contained, but you always looked as if you knew who you were and where you were going."

I scowled. "You're the third person who's told me that. This is really weird. I was suffering through all those years, feeling completely out of it, escaping into books and fantasies because I felt as if everybody else fit in and I was the oddball."

She raised her glass to make her point. "But look, Jo. Look at where all that reading and daydreaming carried you. Right into a terrific, glamorous profession that gives you just the lifestyle you need. You know what? You were right. You didn't fit in. You were a special person with special gifts and talents and you just didn't know it yet. But those things do stick out some way. Other kids pick up on them and respond to them, even though nobody involved actually knows what's going on."

"I admired you back then, too," I said suddenly. "In one way I felt sorry for you because . . . you know . . ."

"I looked like hell." She chuckled.

"Because you looked so miserable, but at the same time you looked—how shall I say it?—hard. Not hard exactly; strong. As if you had a core of something tough that I didn't have. It intimidated me."

I grinned. "And I was right. You did. See? Look what you made out of yourself. Another homely girl without your grit would have just uglied away and had a miserable life. But you were tough. You made a silk purse out of yourself. You won."

"So we were both right in our instincts about each other," she said softly. "What a shame we didn't have the guts to tell each other what we admired, in fifth grade. We might have helped each other tremendously."

"Well, we were just all so scared, back then, Hazel. We all just went around . . . veering off of each other out of our fears about ourselves. We never could get past that. Maybe kids can't. Maybe they aren't unselfish enough at that age to make the effort, make the contact with another person who might or might not reject them and hurt them."

Simultaneously we reached into the popcorn bowl.

"You know," she said, "the worst thing about school, for me, was not having a best friend. I didn't really have a close friend until I got to New York. That was one of the things I envied you for. You were always with Charlotte and Carolyn and Diane and all those. That was why I never went to school dances: because I couldn't get up the courage to walk in alone."

I swallowed my fistful of popcorn and washed it down with the watery end of my last diet Coke.

Sadly I shook my head. "Too soon old, too late smart. I never even liked Charlotte very much. My mother picked her out for me, in the produce department at the grocery store. I went along with that bunch because it was easier and safer than trying to find a genuine friend. Those girls were never important to me. I

133

kept thinking, somewhere in this class there must be somebody I could really talk to, you know, share intimate thoughts with, if I could just figure out who. Charlotte was such a fluff-brain and Carolyn was such a jock, and I was out there in left field. Alone. Heck, you were probably the one I was looking for, and I never . . ."

"We couldn't get past each other's defenses," she said sadly.

/ 10 /

The mountain air was clear, light, pine scented; I threw my head back and drank in lungsful of the wonderful stuff. Beneath me, Pauncho swayed and plodded. The saddle creaked, the curb chain made a soft jingle against his bit. My beat-up old boots caressed my feet in recompense for the aches of dancing in the tight shoes.

His hooves found their way on the narrow, familiar trail without guidance from me. My hands rode easy on the saddle horn.

At the crest of the ridge Pauncho stopped because we always stopped there when we came in from our rides. The narrow valley lay before us: a rambling log house, a storybook blue cottage, a red dust road stitching them together. The western half of the valley was already in deep blue shadow, the air already chilling as it does so suddenly at summer twilight in the mountains.

A dear, familiar shape plodded along the path toward my house. Startling Pauncho into an unaccustomed lope with the heels of my boots, I rode down the slope into the valley, along the pasture fence, and up to the corral. When I slid off him, he took himself indoors and waited by the grain box in hope of another supper.

Theo mashed me in an endless hug. "I saw your car just now when I drove in. I had to run to town for a can of chili for supper. I didn't think you'd be home till around seven."

"It is seven, dummy." I laughed and hugged her harder.

"Well, get the saddle off that animal and come on in. I got the big size chili with the extra-hot sauce. Figured you'd need some real food after all that partying. So? Did you have a good time? On the news last night they told about a plane crashing on takeoff, and I knew it was you, I just knew you were on that flight."

"That happened in Vancouver," I said snidely.

"I know it. Don't confuse me with facts. It was a plane crash, you were away from home, you had to be on that plane. Some guy was out here Saturday looking for property to build on . . ."

She chattered on as I stripped Pauncho of his work clothes and turned him in to the corral. Theo and I walked toward my house, arms around waists.

"I thought we'd have supper at your place," Theo said. "I brought the chili and the nacho crackers, and